For my ...
a small ...
thanks for all the
hard work — and
the listening.

Graham

The Cold Light of Dawn

As dawn breaks on the coast of Brittany, a retired colonel finds the body of an attractive young redhead washed up on the beach.

In the search for her identification the French police pass her picture to the CID at Scotland Yard and it is from there that an enquiry spirals into action. As the facts come in slowly, but surely, Detective Chief Inspector Harry Tipper and his assistant, Charlie Markham, begin to form a picture of the dead woman and her life, and it's a very strange one at that; provoking sympathy on the one hand and revulsion on the other.

The enquiry leads eventually to Whitehall and the highest echelons of the Diplomatic Service, causing the CID to call upon the powers of Special Branch, and even MI5, in their bid to unravel all the strands of this compelling mystery.

Graham Ison, a former policeman himself, has produced a stunning first novel, showing the painstaking thoroughness of a murder enquiry and the logical assembly of evidence. *The Cold Light of Dawn* is a chillingly real tale that will absorb its readers.

THE
COLD LIGHT
OF
DAWN

Graham Ison

MACMILLAN
LONDON

First published in 1988 by
MACMILLAN LONDON LIMITED
4 Little Essex Street London WC2R 3LF
and Basingstoke

Associated companies in Auckland, Delhi, Dublin, Gaborone,
Hamburg, Harare, Hong Kong, Johannesburg, Kuala Lumpur,
Lagos, Manzini, Melbourne, Mexico City, Nairobi, New York,
Singapore and Tokyo

British Library Cataloguing in Publication Data

Ison, Graham
   The cold light of dawn.
   I. Title
   823'.914[F]   PR6059.S6/

   ISBN 0-333-46212-2

Typeset by Matrix, London WC2

Printed and bound in England by Richard Clay Ltd,
Chichester, Sussex

Chapter One

The tall, spare figure of Colonel Pierre Matthieu strode
purposefully along the beach. His erect military carriage
belied his seventy-four years, and had been strengthened
rather than weakened by service in places as disparate as
Normandy, Dien Bien Phu and Algeria. He was every inch
a leader. Every sinew implied a familiarity with command,
with decision, and the personality of a man who possessed
an innate knowledge of what to do in an emergency.

The sun was rising over the hills behind him. To his
right was the sea. Far out, between the two arms of the
cove, little boats bobbed up and down at anchor, their bare
masts pointing to the sky like some strange and wintered
maritime forest. To the south La Cruche d'Or Restaurant
stood on its rocky headland, aloof like its owner, the for-
midable Madame Lebrun.

Behind him, on the road to the fishing port, café keepers,
already astir, had started to set out their chairs and tables on
the pavement, and in the roadway too. Some were planting colourful parasols in the little holes in the tables, but
leaving them folded down for fear of tempting providence
too much.

But Colonel Matthieu saw nothing of this. With a fierce
Gaullist pride in his country, he resented the annual invasion
of holidaymakers, predominantly British, who flooded his
native Brittany; but had to accept, unwillingly, that it was

5

helpful to the economy. As a consequence he did his best to avoid them. Religiously taking his morning constitutional at six o'clock, he stomped along the water's edge, head down, occasionally deviating to avoid the large holes that the previous day's sun-worshippers had dug in the sand as wind-breaks.

His greying Flanders hound, Idol, followed him at a distance of about three metres, keeping pace, occasionally stopping to investigate a piece of jetsam or a strange odour, but always returning to his proper station to the rear of the Colonel, pausing when he did, moving on when he did.

The Colonel knew, the moment he sighted the body, that it was dead. He had seen enough dead bodies in his lifetime to have developed an instinct for death. It lay face down, clad only in bikini briefs, the left arm thrown out above the head, carelessly, revealing the slight bulge of the breast. The chestnut hair was wet and tangled, and the tide, now turning, lapped gently at the shapely thighs, and left little puddles in the white sand around the body.

For a moment or two Colonel Matthieu gazed thoughtfully at the young woman, and then glanced at his dog. '*Garde!*' he said gruffly. The dog, accustomed all his life to military commands, sat on his haunches beside the body.

Colonel Matthieu made his way to the telephone at the end of the esplanade, near the road that led up to the restaurant, and tapped out 17. The gendarme who received the call had been only minutes on duty, but became alert instantly. Not because a dead body had been found, but because the finder was Colonel Matthieu who barked out precise details of what he had found, where he had found it, and the circumstances. Then he added, automatically, a string of instructions to the policeman. Colonel Matthieu could not resist giving orders.

A little while later a van arrived containing two gendarmes. They walked down on to the beach where the Colonel and his dog waited. They looked sceptically at Idol

6

who showed them his teeth and growled until silenced by his owner. Minutes later a small Peugeot police car arrived, a winking blue light on its roof, and the party was joined by the *Maréchal des Logis-Chef*, the non-commissioned officer in charge. The *Chef* saluted the Colonel, then took off his kepi and scratched briefly at his closely cropped head. Although infrequent, drownings were not unknown on this stretch of coast. People got into difficulties while swimming; they fell off yachts; they toppled off cliff tops; but usually the police were already aware that they were missing by the time that their bodies were eventually found. But no one had reported the absence of a shapely young redhead.

The *Chef* surveyed the scene, walking backwards and forwards and around; then he went to his car and made a call on the radio. For ten minutes or so the gendarmes stood around, chatting and smoking their foul cigarettes. Then a police photographer arrived and set up his apparatus, taking pictures of the body from every imaginable angle. The *Chef* issued a string of orders, and the gendarmes dragged the body clear of the water, which had now receded so that it lapped only the ankles, and turned it over. For a moment or two the gendarmes stared at it in reverent silence, one shrugging his shoulders with Gallic regret. They were not awed by death, which they had seen many times, but that a girl so attractive should be lying dead at their feet. Then a blanket was fetched and thrown over it.

One of the gendarmes started making notes. No police force in the world can take any sort of action without writing it all down. He took the Colonel's personal particulars, despite the fact that the gendarme who had received the telephone call had already done so. And then he took a detailed statement of how and when and where the discovery had been made. He even injudiciously enquired the name of the dog, but the *Chef* tutted and waved his hand in a brief gesture of negation. He knew the Colonel, and he knew that the Colonel was starting to show signs of

7

impatience with this petty officialdom. He also knew that the Colonel sometimes talked to Captain Courbet who was the *Chef*'s boss.

Another vehicle arrived – this time a van summoned specially from the mortuary. Two attendants carried a cradle-like stretcher across the sand and placed the body in it with all the ceremony of two men humping a sack of potatoes. Finally, the *Chef* saluted the Colonel and the gendarmes left.

By this time people had started to appear on the sand, some attracted by the activity and the blue lights, others who were intent on an early swim before the now rapidly rising sun became too hot for them. Colonel Matthieu regarded them testily and, growling at his dog, completed his walk. He reached the café and sat down, unfolding the newspaper he had bought on the way, and waited for the coffee and croissants which he had every morning for breakfast, while Idol sat at his feet, drinking from the bowl of water he too had every morning. Every now and then he would pause and glance up at the Colonel wondering if today was the day when he would be given some peanuts, but it was an event which happened rarely.

'You are late this morning, *mon Colonel*,' said the woman who kept the café.

'Yes,' said the Colonel.

The girl's body lay in the mortuary at St Brouille for three days. For three days the gendarmerie waited for someone to inform them of a missing swimmer. No one did.

'I see no alternative but to investigate this death, Givry.' Captain Jules Courbet sat at his desk; he had come to the conclusion with reluctance. 'Here we have the body of a beautiful young woman, arriving on our beaches, and no one claims her.'

'Perhaps she is not from here, Captain,' said the *Maréchal des Logis-Chef*, hopefully. 'Maybe she fell from a yacht in the Golfe de St Malo. There are many yachts in and out of St Malo.'

'So you are now an expert on sailing, eh, *Chef*?'

'It was a thought, that's all.' Givry spread his hands.

'The tides from the Golfe de St Malo would not carry a body here,' said Courbet. He glanced thoughtfully at the plaque on the wall, the plaque of the Yacht-club de St Brouille. The Captain was a sailing enthusiast – a fanatic, Givry thought. All his off-duty hours were spent working on his boat. Occasionally, Givry would say sarcastically, he even sails it. Courbet leaned back in his chair, his gaze fixed on the middle distance, his fingertips together. 'I think that body would have come from Le Roc Dent.'

'But no one goes swimming from the Le Roc Dent, Captain. It is impossible to get into the water – it's a sheer cliff face.'

'But do not forget, *Chef*, that there is a small beach, just to the east. It is possible to swim from there, but easy to get into difficulties. If that happened an ebb-tide would carry the body out, until it met the westward drift of the current, and the incoming tide would bring it in – here, in St Brouille.'

'It is possible, Captain.'

'But I am not an expert on tides, Givry. I just do a little sailing from time to time. We would have to consult an oceanographer who is an expert on this coast.'

'But why, Captain? The girl was drowned swimming. She will have gone for a swim, got into difficulties – it is treacherous here at times.'

'Why not go swimming from the beach here at St Brouille – why go all round to Le Roc Dent, eh?'

'If she did,' said Givry. 'But why has no one come forward to tell us of this missing woman? It is three days, but nothing.'

'And she was found at six o'clock in the morning,' continued Courbet, as if Givry hadn't spoken. 'Which if

9

my theory is correct, would have meant that she went off Le Roc Dent at about nine the previous evening. Almost dark. No one but a fool would go swimming from there at nine o'clock in the evening.'

'Maybe she was a fool,' said Givry. He made the same point again as he had made previously. 'But why has no one told us of this missing girl?'

'Perhaps she was alone here in St Brouille. Many people come on holiday by themselves, *Chef*.'

'But, Captain, she must have been staying somewhere – even if she was alone in a hotel, she would have been missed. It has been in the newspapers, on the radio – on television, even; but not a word.'

'It is a mystery, *Chef* – a mystery.' He shrugged and stood up. 'I suppose we shall have to seek a commission.' He took his kepi from the top of the filing cabinet, flicked a speck of dust from the crown, and put it on.

The *Procureur* was called Philippe Jomard. Now fifty-seven years of age, he had been a rising star in his profession until coming to St Brouille twenty years previously. He had liked the little Brittany town and stayed, refusing all offers of promotion, and the transfers that would have gone with them.

He stood up, moving a wisp of grey hair from his forehead with one hand, extending the other. 'My dear Captain Courbet.' They shook hands. 'You have doubtless come to see me about a certain young lady's body which is an embarrassment to you, yes?'

Courbet nodded. 'Three days, and no one has reported the girl missing.'

The *Procureur* seated himself behind his desk and took out his pen. 'Well, then, Courbet, I suppose we had better start.' He glanced up with a smile. 'A requisition for an autopsy, eh? That is always a good place to start. We shall see what the good Doctor Vernet has to say first, then we

10

shall consider what is to be done next.' He signed the form in front of him and handed it to the gendarmerie captain. 'Do you have time for sailing still?'

'A little,' said Courbet. 'Unfortunately, dead bodies keep getting in the way.'

'That's life,' said the *Procureur*, and laughed. He enjoyed a joke.

Doctor Henri Vernet started his examination by walking slowly round the body on the table. At a desk in the corner sat his secretary, a thin angular woman, who had worked with him for twenty years, and who knew his foibles, his preferences, and above all, knew his moods. Vernet peered closely in the mouth, and at the teeth. He looked at the nostrils, and surveyed the face for some seconds. Then he lifted the arms, examining the armpits, and studying the palms of the hands. Moving down the body, he searched every part, once taking a glass to inspect a scar on the lower abdomen. Then he scrutinised the feet, observing the soles, and probing between the toes. With a dexterity born of a lifetime's practice, he turned the body on to its face, and started again from the head, first searching diligently in the hair, peering minutely at the scalp.

All the time he worked, he talked, sometimes half muttering to himself, so that his secretary's practised ear had to strain to hear what he was saying, as her pencil moved rapidly over the pages of her notebook, recording his every word in her immaculate shorthand.

'Good.' He looked up and acknowledged the gendarme's presence for the first time. 'You have been to an autopsy before?'

'Yes.'

'Good. It is inconvenient to have people fainting all over the place. It's distracting.'

Again he turned the body. Then he walked across to the bench where his instruments were laid out and selected a scalpel. 'Right,' he said, glancing briefly at his secretary. 'Incision – throat to pubis.' Slowly, and with meticulous care, he opened the redhead's body right down the front. The gendarme gulped, breathed deeply, and wished that he could smoke a cigarette, but he knew that that would send Doctor Vernet into a towering rage.

'Vagal inhibition,' said Vernet, in matter-of-fact tones. He noted the look of puzzlement on the face of the *Maréchal des Logis-Chef*. 'It means that the woman was not drowned. . . . '

'But . . . '

Vernet held up a hand. 'Just listen,' he said sharply. 'I do not expect you to understand the scientific details, but in drowning I would expect to find the lungs full of water – that's putting it simply; there are other, more technical reasons for my conclusions. It will all be in my report,' he added, off-handedly. The *Chef* opened his mouth again, but Vernet went on. 'The first reaction would have been that she drowned while swimming, but that is not so. You may have thought,' he said, with a sudden smile, 'that because she was wearing a swimming costume – or half of one – that you had an ordinary accidental death, but someone who goes into the water in a swim-suit expects the water to be cold – they are expecting the shock. If the body had been fully clothed, well. . . . ' He spread his hands. 'Then maybe, yes.'

'What are you saying to me?' asked the *Chef*.

'I am saying that it is not what it seems, that you may have a murder on your hands.' He paused. 'But you are the policeman – not me. There was an English case which I've just been reading.' He tapped a large volume on his desk. 'The Brides-in-the-Bath case, in nineteen-fifteen. A man called Smith waited until his wife was in the bath, then he pulled her sharply by the ankles. When her head went under the water, the water rushed

12

up her nostrils, killing her instantly. It is called vagal inhibition.'

'Could it not have been an accident – this Smith man?'

Vernet smiled. 'I think not. It happened to no less than three of his wives!'

'It looks as though we will have to start an investigation.'

'You are the policeman,' Vernet said again. 'I am only the pathologist; but first you will have to identify the woman. Unless you have done so already?'

'No,' said the *Chef*. 'There is not even a report of such a woman missing.'

Vernet stood up, thrusting his hands into his trousers pockets. 'My report, when it's ready, will contain the approximate age – twenty-eight years, I should think – and a dental chart. There are a few other details – the appendicectomy, and the fact that she has given birth to a child. Beyond that, very little. You have the briefs she was wearing – they may help. It is now your problem, my dear Chef.'

'So we have a murder on our hands?'

'According to Doctor Vernet.' Courbet opened his brief-case and withdrew the pathologist's report. Finding the place on the closely typed page, he said, 'Vagal inhibition is the term he uses. It means that the woman did not drown.'

The *Procureur* nodded. 'I have heard of it before,' he said. 'A paralysis of the central nervous system?'

'Exactly so.'

'Does he say how he thinks it happened?'

Courbet proffered the report to the *Procureur*. 'I have a copy of his report here for you.'

Jomard held up his hand. 'I shall read it later. Perhaps you will just give me the salient facts.'

Courbet outlined what Vernet had already told the *Maréchal des Logis-Chef*, and now set out in greater detail in his report.

'There is very little to go on,' he said in conclusion. 'A pair of briefs – the bottom half of a bikini – but who wears the top half around here?'

'They have a label in them?'

'No label!'

'Ah, that's good.'

'Good?'

'Of course. It shows intent on the part of the murderer to cover his crime. It convinces me that this is a murder.'

'Perhaps they did not have a label to start with,' said Courbet without very much hope that he was right. 'But in any event it makes it harder to identify the woman.'

'What an uninteresting world it would be, my dear Courbet, if everything was easy. Well, we had better start. Captain Jules Courbet . . . ' He spoke as he wrote on the form in front of him. 'Of the Gendarmerie Nationale at St Brouille is hereby granted this *commission rogatoire* to investigate the death of an unknown woman whose body was found at . . . ' He paused and looked up, a quizzical expression on his face. 'Six o'clock in the morning?' Courbet nodded. 'On Monday the twenty-fifth of August, and to bring before me such person or persons who may bear responsibility.' He signed the form and fixed his official seal. 'There, Courbet. Now sit down and have a glass of cognac, and we shall decide what is to be done.'

The investigators of the Gendarmerie Nationale at St Brouille had very little to go on. they had circulated photographs of the dead girl's face, which they would have had to do – crime or not, but there was no response. People who had reported the disappearance of friends or relatives whose description seemed to match that of the girl with the red hair, were interviewed. None identified the body which had so mysteriously appeared on the beach at St Brouille.

The bikini briefs which the girl had been wearing were sent to the forensic science laboratory for examination. All

14

that the scientists could say was that there had been a label once, but it had been cut out, and that the briefs had probably been manufactured in England. That was no great help; since the advent of the Common Market, many English products were on sale in France, and the fact that the woman had been wearing briefs made in England did not necessarily mean that she was English.

At Doctor Vernet's suggestion, the gendarmerie's consultant odontologist examined the dead body's teeth. His findings were much more positive. The dentistry work had, without doubt, he said, been carried out by an English dental surgeon.

'In that case,' said Courbet, 'send a set of her fingerprints to Scotland Yard.'

The result was disappointing. She had not been convicted of any crime in Great Britain, and so her fingerprints were not on record. Neither had the British police any record of a missing person whose description matched that of the girl with red hair.

All the short cuts had failed. There was only one thing left: solid, painstaking and tedious detective work. And it could, and often did, take a very long time. Inspirational detectives, alas, had no place in the real world of crime.

Chapter Two

'The French seem to have got their knickers in a twist over some dead body they found on a beach in Brittany,' said Detective Chief Inspector Harry Tipper. 'Or at least,' he continued, prodding the sealed plastic package with a pencil, 'somebody's knickers.'

'What are we supposed to do with those, then?'

'It might help if you read the report first, Charlie.' Tipper handed his detective sergeant a copy of the French report which had been translated into English by the Interpol office on the floor below.

Charlie Markham read what the French had to say and then looked up. 'What the hell's all this about the Brides-in-the-Bath case – that was years ago, before the First World War I should think.'

'Nearly,' said Tipper. 'Nineteen-fifteen.'

'Well, whenever. What's that got to do with it?'

'It could be a murder – that's what they're getting at. First thing's to try and identify these for them.' Tipper pushed the package towards Markham.

'Some hope,' said Markham. 'According to the report there's not even a label in them.'

'Life's like that. Get them over to the lab and see what they can make of them.'

Doctor Susan Gardiner was the fabrics expert at the Metropolitan Police Forensic Science Laboratory in Lambeth. Although she was still in her early thirties there were few scientists who would argue with her findings, and she had delivered several papers on her subject to learned societies. From an analysis of the bikini briefs, she identified the material and the manufacturer within twenty-four hours. Her report, and the briefs, were returned to Detective Sergeant Markham. The rest was up to the police.

Charlie Markham, who had quite enough work of his own, had no great enthusiasm for helping the French police solve a suspicious death. He made several telephone calls, and one or two visits. The sum total of his exertions was to discover that the briefs were one half of a bikini sold widely in the south-east mainly at multiple outlets. The chances of finding out who had purchased that particular bikini were so remote that he didn't even try.

Some aspects of criminal investigation are better classified as calculated guesswork, and the fact that the bikini in question was likely to have been sold in south-east England, caused Tipper to believe that the purchaser might live there. It was a short cut. It would be Tipper's luck for the woman to have travelled to London from Scotland just once, and to have been awkward enough to buy a bikini on that one visit. Nevertheless, he circulated her photograph in *Confidential Informations*, a police-only publication circulated to all forces in the south-east, in the hope that it might produce an identification. He also asked the General Dental Council to circularise their practitioners, sending a copy of the chart prepared by the gendarmerie odontologist.

'Cracked it, sir,' said Charlie Markham, three weeks later. Harry Tipper looked up. 'Penelope Lambert, she's called. Got an address in Wimbledon.'

'And?'

'And nothing, sir – not yet.'

17

'Well you'd better get down there – see what you can find out.'

'I was just going.' Markham looked hurt.

'Miss or Mrs?'

'Mrs.'

'Well she might have a husband sitting there, wondering where the hell she is. Anyway, if it is a murder, the French'd like to know a bit more than her name and address.'

'I suppose so,' said Markham, looking put upon. With the discovery of the dead redhead's identity he had hoped that that was the last he'd be bothered with her. It rather looked as though he was only just beginning.

It was a large Victorian house in Wimbledon which had been converted into flats. There was no response when Markham pressed the bell-push marked 'Lambert' at the front door. He knew that there wouldn't be. He already had that sort of feeling about this enquiry. He tried another marked 'Mason', and eventually a woman's voice crackled through the intercom, asking who was there. Clearly unhappy about the single word 'Police', she opened the front door a fraction on the chain.

Markham held up his warrant card. 'Good morning, madam. Police, New Scotland Yard.'

Reluctantly satisfied, the woman released the chain and admitted him to the hallway.

'I'm making enquiries about a Mrs Penelope Lambert.'

'She lives upstairs.'

'Yes,' he said, 'so I believe.' He nodded to the open door of the woman's flat. 'I wonder if I might come in and talk to you?'

'She's away, you know.'

'Yes, I know.' He paused. 'It's Mrs Mason, is it?'

'Yes – Letitia Mason.' She said it as though he ought to recognise the name. 'Won't you sit down? I expect you'd like a cup of tea, wouldn't you? I know policemen usually do.'

'Well, that's very kind, but I don't want to put you to any trouble.' Charlie Markham would actually have preferred a Scotch, but Mrs Mason didn't look like someone who'd have a bottle tucked away.

'Oh, it's no trouble, Mr . . . ?'

'Markham – Detective Sergeant Markham, and thank you.'

The room was what Markham's mother would have described as chintzy. Cluttered with ornaments, flowery loose covers on the three-piece suite, and photographs and pictures, all of which seemed to contain depictions of ballet dancers.

Mrs Mason set down the tray on a side-table. Even that went with the room: a lace tray-cloth, and flowered china. 'I see you're admiring my pictures, Sergeant.'

'I take it you're a ballet enthusiast?'

'I'm a ballet mistress,' said Mrs Mason, 'and I bet you I can still kick higher than you, even though I can probably give you ten years. Do you take sugar and milk?'

'Do you know, by any chance, if Mrs Lambert's husband is likely to be home later – or perhaps you know where he works?'

Mrs Mason looked up sharply. 'She doesn't have a husband. She's divorced. Why d'you want to know?'

Markham took a photograph from his pocket. 'Would you take a look at that, Mrs Mason, please.'

She stared at it for some seconds. 'Yes, that's her. It's not very good of her though, she's much prettier than that.'

'It's a passport photograph,' said Markham. 'They're never very good.' The first thing that Tipper had done was to get a copy from the Passport Office; he knew from experience that a photograph of a corpse tended to upset witnesses. 'I'm afraid that Mrs Lambert is dead, Mrs Mason.'

Letitia Mason set her cup and saucer down carefully on the occasional table at her side. 'Oh, no!' she said. 'The poor girl – how dreadful. What happened?'

19

'She was drowned – in France; in Brittany as a matter of fact.' There was no point at this stage in telling this woman that the police were regarding it as a suspicious death.

'How awful. I knew she was going away, but I didn't know where – or for how long. She didn't say.'

'And how long has she been away?'

Mrs Mason pondered for a moment. 'It must be getting on for five weeks, I suppose. Actually I was beginning to get a little worried, although she tended to go away quite often. Her job, she said.'

'Which was?'

'Pardon?'

'What was her job?'

'Oh, I'm sorry, yes. She worked at the Foreign Office.'

'Really? In what capacity, do you know?'

'Not exactly, but I got the impression she wasn't a typist or anything like that. She never talked about her work. Well she wouldn't, would she, not doing something like that? But she would mention when she was going off to a conference – sometimes it was abroad. She used to tell me that she wanted to be stationed overseas; in an embassy in some exotic place. She used to joke about it and say that with her luck it would probably be somewhere quite awful.'

'Did she say where she was going this time?'

'No – she didn't – other than to say she was going on holiday.'

'You say she was divorced; did you know anything about her ex-husband?'

'Well I'm not one to pry, Sergeant, but she did tell me things from time to time, and you can't stop people talking, can you?'

Fortunately no, thought Markham.

'She would come down here sometimes,' continued Mrs Mason. 'In the evenings – we'd have a cup of something, or occasionally even a glass of sherry.' She wrinkled her nose and smiled as though she was revealing something excessively naughty. 'And she would sit there, where you're sitting, and chat away. I think she was lonely, you know. Of course, she'd had a lot of tragedy in her life, even though she was only a young girl.'

'Tragedy?'

'Oh yes. There was the child. They had a son, she and her husband, and the poor little mite was drowned . . . ' She paused. 'That's ironic, isn't it? It was in a swimming pool, at a friend's house. She'd been over for a cup of tea and a chat, I suppose. This friend had a big house and a swimming pool in the garden. Apparently he'd strayed off – you know what children are like – and he fell in the pool and drowned. It must have been awful for her. You can't let them out of your sight for a minute, and I should know – I had two. That's my eldest.' She pointed at a photograph that stood on the television. 'Of course, he's nearly forty now . . . '

'And that was the cause of the break-up?' He brought her back on course.

'What? Oh, yes, I suppose so. It was so unfair really. Just when she needed support he abandoned her – so cruel. But men are like that, at least in my experience. I had the same problem. My husband ran off with some young thing in the *corps de ballet* who fluttered her eyelashes at him.'

'I didn't think the world of ballet was like that,' said Markham.

'Oh, you'd be surprised, Sergeant. A big strong ballet dancer will pick them up and throw them around – you'd be amazed the effect that has on some girls. Ballerinas are no different to anyone else – some of them will run after anything in tights. Well they can see what they're getting, can't they?' She suddenly put her hand to her mouth and coloured slightly. 'Oh, I'm so sorry, that wasn't a very lady-like remark, was it?'

Markham smiled. Mrs Mason was turning out to be something of an enigma; perhaps she did have a bottle of

21

Scotch tucked away somewhere. 'You were saying – about Mrs Lambert . . . '

'Yes, well this husband apparently turned on her. And she so desperately wanted a family, you know. What a waste – such a lovely young girl. But that was that. They split up and got divorced.'

'Did she have any boy friends?'

'Oh, I think so. She never talked about them – not directly. She'd sometimes mention that she'd been out somewhere nice for dinner – that sort of thing. And she'd occasionally be brought home in someone's car – or in a taxi. I never asked her about them, naturally. I mean, it wasn't my place to.' Letitia Mason pointed suddenly across the room. 'She bought me that on one occasion for looking after her flat.'

Markham's gaze followed her extended finger. She was pointing at a china figurine of a ballerina in a place of honour on the mantelshelf.

'I told her it was much too expensive. I know what these things cost; but she said that she wasn't short of money. I can only assume that the divorce settlement left her reasonably well off – no more than she deserved, poor child. Her husband was an absolute swine, by all accounts.'

'She left you her keys on this occasion, I presume, Mrs Mason?'

'Yes, yes she did.'

'I need to examine her flat, you see.'

'Oh! Well I suppose that's all right.'

'Did she have any relatives – anyone she mentioned?'

'No, she didn't. Strange that, but I got the impression that there were some parts of her life she never mentioned. I really don't know.' Mrs Mason sounded as though she had failed in some way. 'I've got the keys in my bag – I'll get them. Do you want me to come up with you?'

'No thank you, Mrs Mason, that won't be necessary.

You've been most helpful, and I mustn't take up any more of your time.'

'Oh, it's no trouble. I don't get many visitors.'

'I may need to talk to you again, Mrs Mason.'

'Of course, Sergeant – any time at all. Oh, by the way . . . ' She paused. 'Do you know anything about the funeral arrangements? She was such a lovely girl,' she said again. 'I really would like to go.'

'No I don't. You see her body is in France still, so it may be some time. But I will let you know. One other thing. Do you know if Mrs Lambert had a car?'

'Yes, she did – a little silver thing, Japanese, I think. Here, I'll show you – it's outside.' She walked to the window and drew aside the net curtain. 'There – there it is.'

'Thank you,' said Markham. 'You've been most helpful – and thank you for the tea.'

Charlie Markham didn't really know what he was looking for. The flat consisted of a sitting-room on the front of the house, a bedroom, a bathroom and a kitchenette. He started from the middle of the sitting-room, surveying and absorbing. He wondered whether he ought to be searching at all – at this stage, anyway. The place would have to be gone over by a scenes-of-crime officer, given that this was supposed to be a murder – possibly, and he might do more harm than good if he started messing about now. He shrugged his shoulders. He knew what he was doing. With twenty years service behind him, and involvement in more murders than most people had had hot breakfasts – and that included a fair few of his senior officers – he thought that a preliminary examination would do no harm.

On the unremarkable grey fitted carpet stood a natural pine three-piece suite with the sort of canvas upholstery that abounds in shops in Chelsea and Hampstead. Just as common in such shops was the black ash bookcase and cabinet that stood against the wall opposite the door.

23

But it was the secretaire, just to Markham's left, that was likely to prove the most interesting. It was unlocked and he moved the dining-chair next to it so that he could sit down.

It was at that moment that the telephone rang, so harshly that it made Markham jump, and he swore.

'Charlie?'

'Yes,' said Markham defensively.

'It's Tipper here.'

'Blimey, guv'nor, you nearly scared the life out of me.'

'How're you getting on?'

'Just got into the flat – about to have a poke about, as a matter of fact.'

'Well don't – just leave it until we get a team down to do the complete business.'

'What . . . ?'

'I've just got the result of your enquiry from the DHSS at Newcastle.'

'And?'

'Penelope Lambert worked for the Foreign Office.'

'I know,' said Markham. 'The woman in the flat downstairs told me. Why? Does it matter?'

'It may have no bearing on her death,' continued Tipper, 'but then again, it might. If there is something more sinister in this, we want to do it right from the beginning.'

'D'you want me to hang on here, then?'

'Yes – I'll see you shortly.'

Within the hour Harry Tipper had arrived at Wimbledon, together with a scenes-of-crime officer, a fingerprint man, and the inevitable photographer.

'Anything of interest?'

'Not as far as I can see. Just an ordinary sort of pad. If there's going to be anything, it'll be among that lot, I should think.' Markham pointed at the secretaire. 'There's all sorts of stuff in there. Loads of papers, bills, letters – that sort of thing.'

Tipper pouted. 'Wrap it up and bring it with you. If you start going through it now you'll be here for ages.'

'There's a car, guv'nor,' said Markham. 'Outside in the street. I suppose we'd better have a look at that.'

'How long's it been there? Since she went away?'

'I suppose so.'

'I'll get the SOCO to take a look,' said Tipper, and called the scenes-of-crime officer over. 'You'd better get on to traffic division, Charlie, and get a unit up here to open it up for us. It must be locked or someone'd've nicked it ages ago. Surprised they haven't anyway.'

The traffic division PC made short work of entering Penelope Lambert's car, and waited while Markham had what he called a poke about inside. The only thing he found that was likely to be of any interest was a diary in the glove compartment.

'Funny place to keep a diary,' he said.

'Funny things, women,' said Tipper with feeling, and turning to the traffic officer, said, 'Put a wheel on that and get it down to the nick, will you? It's to be preserved for fingerprints.'

Most of the fingerprints found in Penelope Lambert's flat, and all of those in her car, proved, not surprisingly, to be hers. After a comparison with the impressions taken by the gendarmerie from the girl's body – and a few uncomplimentary remarks about their quality – the Yard's fingerprint officers had eventually agreed, with the customary reluctance of experts to commit themselves, that they were identical.

Mrs Mason had been persuaded to provide a set of her fingerprints for elimination purposes, and they proved that the ballet mistress in the flat downstairs had done more than just look into the flat on occasions to make sure that everything was all right. She had taken a great interest in her neighbour's affairs, and had clearly let her curiosity get the better of her when confronted with the secretaire, the wardrobe, and the drawers of the dressing-table. Tipper determined not to mention it to her – at least not immediately; there might be an occasion when it would come in useful.

But there were other prints too. Tipper and Markham automatically, and with typical policemen's cynicism, assumed that they belonged to men friends. Mrs Mason however, was unable to confirm that this was the case, merely repeating what she had told Markham, that occasionally Mrs Lambert had talked of going out to dinner 'somewhere nice', but without elaborating upon the company in which she had done so. Mrs Mason also reiterated that she wasn't one to pry into her neighbour's affairs.

'Did Mrs Lambert say anything about leaving her job?' Tipper had asked, during the course of the interview. One of the gratuitous pieces of information that the Department of Health and Social Security had furnished was the fact that Penelope Lambert had left the employ of the Foreign and Commonwealth Office on the twenty-second of August – the day upon which Mrs Mason said she had gone on holiday – a mere three days before her body had been found, washed up on a Brittany beach.

It was all a little too neat for Tipper. 'Make an appointment for us to see the security officer at the Foreign Office, Charlie, will you – probably an ex-copper in that job, which'll be handy.'

The official they saw was not a retired policeman, but a career Foreign Office man, and he was very helpful. He produced Mrs Lambert's file and drew Tipper's attention to the fact that the last few folios dealt with her resignation.

'Do you think her death may have had anything to do with the fact that she was employed here at F and CO?' he asked.

'Your guess is as good as mine,' said Tipper. 'But I must

admit that the thought had crossed my mind. D'you think that I might borrow her letter of resignation?'

'Most certainly – provided you give me a receipt for it, and perhaps I could take a photocopy first, just in case we need to refer to it.'

'It might seem a bit late in the day,' said Tipper, producing a plastic sleeve from his brief-case, 'but may I put the letter in this before you handle it any more?'

The security officer looked slightly puzzled. 'Of course,' he said, a half-smile on his face, 'but why?'

'I want to have it examined for fingerprints.'

'What, on paper? I didn't realise that you could take fingerprints off paper.'

'Good,' said Tipper smiling. 'The fewer people who know, the better. Incidentally, I should be grateful if you didn't mention my visit to anyone here, or the reason for it.'

'Your secret's safe with me, Chief Inspector. There is nothing different about the Foreign Office, you know. Regrettably we have the same number of thieves, *habitués* of men's toilets, and people who lose important documents as most other departments in Whitehall seem to have.' He stood up, extending a hand. 'If there is anything else I can do to assist, don't hesitate to get in touch.'

A senior fingerprint officer came to see Harry Tipper. He laid Penelope Lambert's letter of resignation on the Detective Chief Inspector's desk. 'I don't know what you're going to make of this, Harry,' he said. 'But there are about five different sets of marks on that, but not one of them belongs to Penelope Lambert.'

'You've got that look about you that says you've got something else up your sleeve.'

The fingerprint officer smiled. 'One of the sets on the letter matches one of the unidentified sets we found in her flat.'

'Thanks,' said Tipper cynically.

27

The flying time from Gatwick to St Jacques Airport in Rennes was about two hours. Tipper had persuaded his commander that a liaison visit to the Gendarmerie Nationale was essential. Colin Finch had agreed.

The aircraft stopped and Tipper and Markham descended the steps to be met by Captain Jules Courbet in uniform. That was a surprise; in England criminal investigation was always carried out by officers in plain clothes. They were to learn, however, that in France a gendarme has authority to carry out enquiries only if he is clothed in the livery of the Republic.

'Mr Tipper, yes?' Courbet extended a hand.

'Yes, but Harry's the name.'

'Good – and this?' He gestured towards Markham.

'Charlie Markham – my Detective Sergeant.'

'So – Charlie. Welcome to France.'

They drove the forty-odd miles to St Brouille in a gendarmerie Citroën with its blue light lazily revolving, but with no other indication of urgency. Courbet insisted that, as a preamble, they have lunch and a couple of bottles of good French wine just to get them in the right mood for the afternoon's work.

They settled, finally, in Courbet's office at St Brouille, and he outlined what they had done so far.

'We are aware of the identification, Harry, and we are most grateful for that. It seems that the girl Mrs Lambert – was on holiday here, but we have been unable to trace yet where she was staying.' He paused in thought. 'Assuming, of course, that she was staying in St Brouille. You must realise, naturally, that this is a popular part of France for holidaymakers – we have thousands every year. Givry here, my *Chef* . . . ' He indicated the *Maréchal des Logis-Chef* with a wave of the hand. 'He has worked very hard, making enquiries at hotels, at *gîtes*, and at *logis* in and around the area in an effort to discover whether such a woman was here. We have made enquiries all over, but to no avail. Even camping sites, but nothing. Until we can discover where she was, enquiries about anyone who may have been with her are impossible.'

'There is a complication, Jules.' Tipper pronounced his name as though he was describing precious stones. 'Mrs Lambert worked for our Foreign Office. We are wondering whether that made any difference – whether it complicates matters at all. It is possible, I suppose, that it had something to do with her death.'

Courbet shrugged his shoulders. 'It is possible, yes. But what I do not know.'

Tipper and Markham returned to London reinforced by some good wine, the certain knowledge that policemen of all nations get on well together, but very little else.

'I think,' said Tipper, 'that we must start at the Foreign Office. And I reckon that the bloke she worked for is not a bad place to start.'

Chapter Three

'Mr Mallory will see you now.' The tall girl with the plummy accent clearly regarded policemen as rather strange – the sort of persons one did not normally see in the rarefied atmosphere of the Foreign Office in Whitehall.

Mallory was smooth. Immaculately dressed, he exuded a charm that was effortless – part of being a diplomat. 'Chief Inspector,' he said, rising from his desk and walking towards Tipper with his hand outstretched. 'Come in – do take a seat.' He nodded towards Markham. 'Sergeant,' he said, in little more than a murmur, instantly recognising him as Tipper's subordinate and letting him know that he knew.

He conducted the two policemen to a small circle of easy chairs in one corner of his large office – what he called his conference area – and lowered himself gracefully into one of them. 'What can I do to help you?'

'Mrs Penelope Lambert's death,' said Tipper without preamble.

'I saw it in the newspapers – a tragedy.' Mallory sat with one elbow over the back of his chair, absently playing with his signet ring. 'She was drowned, I understand? On holiday.'

'On holiday, Mr Mallory – why do you say that?'

Mallory appeared slightly disconcerted. 'Well, surely . . . ?'

'I believe that Mrs Lambert had resigned her post here – as your secretary.'

'Yes indeed, about, oh – five weeks ago, I suppose it must have been.'

'Why?'

'I don't quite understand . . . '

'Why did she resign, Mr Mallory?'

'I'm afraid I don't know.'

'Did she not say? In my experience, a secretary is usually fairly open with the man she works for. Did she not put forward any reason?'

'No, she didn't. I presumed that she had something else to go to.'

'Sudden was it?' Tipper knew that she had asked to be allowed to resign without the usual period of notice from his chat with the security chief.

'Well I suppose it was, but young women are often unpredictable, aren't they? I have to admit, Chief Inspector, that I didn't really put it to her. Incidentally, may I ask why the police are taking such an interest in Mrs Lambert's death? Surely it was a straightforward accidental drowning – albeit a tragedy?'

Tipper smiled disarmingly. 'In a sense, Mr Mallory, we are acting as agents for the French police. They are conducting the enquiry into her death. I suppose other police forces – other judicial systems – have different ways of doing things. The fact that she had worked here until quite recently might have led them to think that there could be international ramifications.' He met Mallory's gaze. 'But being in the Foreign Office, I suppose you'd know that better than me?'

'Quite so, Chief Inspector. Of course.'

'How long had she been your secretary?'

Mallory looked across his office, beyond the two policemen. 'Two years – perhaps slightly longer.'

'What can you tell me about her – Mrs Lambert the person?'

'In what way?' Mallory clearly wasn't going to be an easy man to interview.

'Something about her background might help.'

'Divorced – but you probably know that already.'

Tipper nodded, and Mallory continued. 'Apparently she and her husband had a child six or seven years ago, and the child died – an accident I believe. That, I gather, is what started the break-up of the marriage. There were mutual recriminations – arguments about the apportionment of blame – that sort of thing. Anyway, they split up and finally divorced. There was no one else as far as I know.'

'I understand that she had only recently moved to Wimbledon?'

'So I believe. She lived in Hampton Wick before that, but she was always complaining about the trains. I think she moved so that she would be near the Underground. Much easier for the office.'

'You seem to know quite a lot about your late secretary, Mr Mallory.'

Mallory smiled condescendingly. 'I always take an interest in my staff, Chief Inspector. It's part of good management, I always think.'

'And yet you have no idea why she resigned, or what she intended to do?'

Mallory looked sharply at Tipper. 'No – no idea at all.' Tipper remained passive, willing the man opposite him to continue. 'It was all rather sudden,' said Mallory eventually. 'She just put her notice in one morning, and that was that. She even asked if the usual period of notice could be dispensed with.'

'Strange,' said Tipper. 'Just like that.'

'As you say, Chief Inspector – just like that. But then women do some strange things at times, don't you find? Are you married?'

'Yes,' said Tipper. 'And you?'

'Oh yes, very much so.' He glanced at his watch. 'Well, gentlemen, unless there is anything else – I do have an appointment with the Minister.'

'Thank you, Mr Mallory. I think that's all – for the time being.' Mallory looked vaguely disconcerted at that. 'Oh, there's just one other thing,' said Tipper, as he reached the door. 'Did Mrs Lambert hand her notice to you?'

'Er, no.' Mallory put a hand to his face and gently massaged the temple with his middle finger. 'As I recall, she handed it straight to the Establishments people. She mentioned it to me, naturally, but almost in passing. I thought it a bit strange.'

'Well?' Tipper looked at Charlie Markham, relaxed in an armchair on the other side of the office.

'Nasty piece of work. Don't fancy him at all, sir.'

Tipper parted the slats of the venetian blind and stared down into Broadway, sixteen floors below. He continued talking with his back towards Markham. 'How old d'you reckon he was, Charlie?'

'About forty-six – forty-seven perhaps. Find out, easily enough, I suppose. Why? Does he interest you, guv'nor?'

Tipper turned from the window. 'Yes, Charlie, he does. It wouldn't surprise me to find that he was having an affair with the gorgeous Mrs Lambert.'

'But what about the set of fingerprints on her letter of resignation that C3 also found in her flat? Surely the owner of those is a better bet?'

'Might be his, Charlie.'

'But he didn't handle that letter – it went straight to the Establishments people.'

'So he said, Charlie, so he said.'

Markham nodded slowly. 'As you say, sir, so he said.'

'Devote a little attention to him. See what you can find out about him. Where he lives – what his wife's like, all that sort of thing. And above all does anyone know if he was having it off with Penelope. But be careful how you go. I don't want him to think we're taking an interest.

And that place ... ' He waved in the direction of the Foreign Office on the other side of St James's Park. 'That place is a hotbed of gossip and rumour, I should think. You'll probably learn a lot, but it could easily get back to him, and I don't want him alerted, just in case.'

Charlie Markham was a good detective. He knew that any attempt on his part to penetrate the bastion of the Foreign and Commonwealth Office was doomed to fail, particularly as it was, by its very nature, a security-conscious organisation. But Charlie Markham also knew women. And he decided to make a play for the girl who now occupied the late Mrs Lambert's chair as Mallory's new secretary. Plummy and refined she might be, but Charlie's South London approach had won over similar girls on two or three occasions in the past – and when he wasn't really trying. Apart from anything else, he knew damned well that her curiosity would get the better of her, either way, by which he meant that if Mallory had told her why the police had called, she would be curious, and if he hadn't told her, she'd be even more inquisitive.

The trouble with the Foreign Office is that it is a sprawling rabbit warren of a place with several entrances. It was four or five days before Markham sighted the girl leaving by the King Charles Street exit.

'How funny,' said Markham, spreading his arms expansively.

For a moment the girl looked perplexed; she knew the face but wasn't sure why. Then it registered. 'Oh, you're the policeman who came to see Mr Mallory.'

'Absolutely right,' said Markham. 'And I was just coming to see you, but here you are sloping off home. You finish early.' He made it sound like an accusation and glanced at his watch. 'Only a quarter to five – what a wicked waste of the taxpayers' money.'

She smiled coyly; Markham's bluffness was a bit over-whelming, but he was relying on it. 'These class birds like a bit of rough,' he had said many times before.

'Er look, I suppose . . . ' Markham contrived to look momentarily indecisive. 'I was hoping to pop in for a quick word, but . . . '

'I shall be in the office tomorrow morning,' she said helpfully.

'Ah, but I shan't – up at the Bailey all day.' He paused again. 'Look, how about a quick drink, unless your hus-band's waiting for his dinner?'

'I'm not married, but . . . ' She looked doubtful.

'I don't want to take you out of your way,' said Charlie. 'Or are you going home to wash your hair?' He laughed as he said it and the girl joined in.

He steered her to a corner table in one of Whitehall's pubs. 'What is your pleasure, marm?' he asked with staged gallantry.

'Could I have a gin-and-tonic, please?'

'You most certainly may.'

He put her drink on the table and set down his own Scotch. 'I'm Charlie Markham, in case you've forgotten,' he said, 'but I don't know your name.' Hurriedly he added, in an exaggerated whisper, 'but don't shout it or they'll think I've just picked you up.'

She laughed, 'Well you have, haven't you. I'm Kate McLaren.'

He extended a hand, taking hers. 'Pleased to meet you Kate.'

She sipped at her drink, and put it back on the table. 'Well?' She raised her eyebrows.

He offered her a cigarette, but she declined. 'Do you mind if I do?'

'No, but it's very bad for you.'

'I know,' said Markham, 'and I've had all the lectures.' He stretched his legs out straight and took a mouthful of

Scotch. 'I was wondering,' he said. 'How well did you know Penelope Lambert?'

'Not at all.'

'Oh!'

'Did you expect me to, then?'

'Well, as you'd taken over her job, I thought perhaps . . . '

'No, I was in another section. I just got transferred. Mrs Lambert apparently left quite suddenly.'

'Does that often happen?'

'Quite a lot actually. The F and CO are such poor payers – compared with outside that is. A secretary in the West End can often get half as much again.'

'Why do you stay then? I mean why do any of you stay?'

'The glamour, I suppose.' She gave a wry little smile.

'What glamour? There's not much glamour attached to a typewriter – and I know; I've hammered one often enough.'

'It's the chance of foreign travel, I suppose. There's always the possibility of an overseas posting – in some exotic faraway place.'

'Like downtown Djibouti, for instance?'

'Now you're making fun of me.' She wrinkled her nose. 'It's a chance you take. I suppose we all hope for the Caribbean, or the States, or Tokyo – somewhere like that, but— '

'But at the end of the day it's bashing a typewriter in some office somewhere.'

'Yes, I suppose you're right.'

'Funny bloke, your guv'nor,' said Markham, deliberately drifting nearer his target.

'What, Mr Mallory?'

'Yes,' Markham stared into the middle distance, apparently musing. 'Arthur Mallory . . . '

'It's not Arthur – it's Robert.'

'Oh, is it? I thought it was Arthur. Don't know why. Just had this idea in the back of my mind.'

36

'Soon to be *Sir* Robert.'

'Really?'

She looked guilty, as if she had just disclosed some state secret. 'Well I don't know for sure, but you can more or less tell when everyone's due, and he must be near the top of the list. I should think he'll be off soon.'

'Off?'

'Well he must be due for an ambassadorship shortly.'

'Mmmm!' Markham raised his eyebrows. 'I didn't realise he was that important.'

'Oh he's been one before. But that's how they work. They have to come back for a few years here and there. Just to keep in touch, I suppose. He's very young; what they call a high flier.'

'I wonder what his wife thinks of that.' He looked searchingly at the girl. 'I suppose he's married?'

'Oh, yes. They mostly are. As a matter of fact I can't think of any unmarried ambassadors.'

'But it must make for problems – things like buying and selling houses for instance.'

'I think they let them out.' Kate finished her drink and looked at her watch.

'Let me get you another – one for the road?'

She looked doubtful. 'Well, just one. Then I must fly.'

'To Djibouti?' He smiled as he took their glasses towards the bar.

'You were saying – he's going to let his house,' said Markham, making a presumption. 'Where does he live?'

'Chalfont St Giles, I think – yes, I'm sure.' A look of doubt crossed her face. 'You seem awfully interested in Mr Mallory.'

'Not really,' said Markham. 'Come to think of it, I should think he's a pretty uninteresting sort of bloke. I don't suppose he even chats up his secretary.'

She took a sip of her drink and placed it carefully on the table again. 'Don't you be too sure about that,' she said.

'Well, well!' said Markham. He was hoping that she was unused to drinking and that the gin was going to her head. He was wrong.

'He's taken me out for a drink a couple of times, and once to lunch. And I've only been there just over four weeks. It's usually when we've been working fairly hard. When we've had to get a special brief out – something of that sort. But that's the FCO.' She smiled, but wasn't looking at the policeman when she did so.

'And there's punters like me thinking it's all pretty heavy stuff at the Foreign Office.'

'Punter?' Kate looked genuinely mystified.

'It means,' said Markham, with Cockney clarity, 'the innocents of this world who will be taken in by anything.' He paused. 'Like me.'

She didn't smile, but looked at him levelly. 'I don't see you being taken in by anything, quite frankly.'

'Well – perhaps not often, except by a pretty girl. 'Nother drink?'

'No, thank you. I really must go.'

Looking as if the thought had just that moment occurred to him, Markham said, 'How about a bite one evening?'

'A bite?'

'Yeah – a bit of dinner. There's a very good Italian not a million miles from here.'

She looked doubtful. 'Maybe.'

'At least I know your 'phone number,' he said with a chuckle. Markham still had his eye to the main task, but had never been known to overlook any fringe benefits that arose. 'I'll be in touch.' And he shepherded her towards the door.

'There's an entry in her diary for June the seventeenth,' said Markham. He walked through the door of Tipper's office as he spoke and stopped in front of the DCI's desk.

Tipper looked up expectantly, but Markham continued to read the small book in his hand.

'Well get on with it, Charlie, for God's sake.'

Markham looked up. 'Er, yes, sorry. It says "J took photographs".'

'Who's "J"?'

'Search me, guv.'

'And what's more to the point, Charlie, what sort of photographs?'

'No idea.'

'How thoroughly has the flat been searched?'

'With a fine toothcomb.'

'And?'

'No photographs. At least not what you'd call compromising. There's the usual family things – holidays, and so on. Quite a few of a child, and groups of Mrs Lambert, the child and a bloke.'

'That'll be her ex, I suppose. Incidentally, how are we getting on with tracing him?'

'Came across an address in South Woodford, but he's not there. Enquiries, as they say, are continuing.'

'What's his name?'

'James Lambert. He seems to have been in the computer business – salesman, I think.'

'He could be "J" then? I wonder if he took these photographs.'

'I doubt it somehow. From what Mrs Mason said it was a bit of an acrimonious divorce.' Markham continued to thumb through the diary. 'There's nothing else of any consequence in here. Usual things like hairdressing appointments, dentist, and so on, but no more about photographs.'

'Be interesting to see those. If they were sufficiently important for her to make a note of it in her diary, they could be quite significant.'

Markham laughed. 'Not half. And if they're that interesting she won't have them, will she? He'll have kept them.'

'Or her.'

'Her – what Penelope?'

'No. We're assuming that "J" is a bloke, just as you've assumed that these photographs are pornographic. It could have been a girl who took them.'

'What a nasty mind you've got, guv,' said Markham.

They eventually traced James Lambert to a flat in Battersea. He was about thirty-five years of age with greying hair and a moustache in the Che Guevara style that had been fashionable in the seventies. His attitude, at least in the beginning, was hostile, and it was with some reluctance that he admitted the policemen to the flat at all.

'What's this all about?' he asked aggressively.

'I understand you were once married to Mrs Penelope Lambert?'

'Yes.'

'And the marriage ended in divorce.'

'Yes. A lot of marriages do. What's that got to do with the police?'

'Mrs Lambert is dead, I'm afraid.'

'Oh!' He mellowed slightly. 'I'm sorry to hear that. But she really didn't mean anything to me – not any more. Well thanks for coming to tell me.' He spoke grudgingly and made a move towards the door.

'There's more to it than that, Mr Lambert,' said Tipper, remaining impassively where he was. 'She was murdered.'

'Christ!' Lambert sat down suddenly. The two policemen also sat down, uninvited.

'Perhaps you would tell us when you last saw your ex-wife.'

'About two years ago I should think. A bit less perhaps. Bumped into her in Regent Street – round about the Christmas before last, it must have been. We just exchanged pleasantries, which was unusual for us, and went our respective ways.'

'Why did you split up?'

'Why are you asking?'

'Because we're trying to find out who killed her. If there was another man, that may be relevant.'

'There was another man – several in fact,' said Lambert bitterly, 'but that, oddly enough, wasn't the reason for the split. It was the boy.' He looked up, staring directly at Tipper. 'We had a son, Mark. She went to see a friend of hers one afternoon, and the kiddy fell into their swimming pool and drowned.' His hands were linked together, tightly clenched. 'If that bitch had kept her eye on him he would have been here today. He'd have been seven now.'

'So you got divorced?'

'Yes.'

'Is there anything else you want to tell us?'

Lambert looked from one detective to the other. 'It's easy to be wise with hindsight, I suppose, but we shouldn't have got married in the first place. She was a very attractive girl, and she was an easy lay. Trouble was she carried on being one even after we were married. I think that even if we hadn't lost Mark it wouldn't have lasted. That just speeded things up, really.' Lambert was more relaxed now, more willing to talk, as though he was relieved at being able to unburden himself. 'She was a bitch, you know – a real bitch.'

Tipper said nothing. He knew from experience that once a witness started to talk, as Lambert was now doing, he was inclined to go on – often further than he intended.

'And it's nearly two years since you saw her?' It was Markham who spoke.

'That's what I said.'

'You didn't see her in June of this year?'

'No. And I don't care if I never see her again.'

'You won't,' said Tipper softly.

'Eh? Oh no, of course not – sorry.'

'Where did you meet your wife, Mr Lambert?'

'Ex-wife,' Lambert corrected him. 'At a party at a friend's

place. It was one of those things you do when you're younger. A few drinks, a few birds, and, with a bit of luck in bed by ten.' He smiled, a rare flash of humour. 'If you're not – go home.'

'And were you?'

'In bed? Yes. We just seemed to hit it off. She was about twenty – twenty-one, perhaps, and was starting off in modelling. She'd done a commercial course of some kind, but that wasn't for her. Too mundane, she said.' He took out a packet of cigarettes and lighted one without offering them to either of the policemen. 'She was adamant that she was going to succeed, too. But then she was as hard as nails – something I didn't find out until after our marriage.'

'And how long afterwards did you get married?'

'Oh, a couple of months. Much too quick, really. It was then that I started to find out what she was really like. We had Mark almost immediately, and that did it. She hated domestic drudgery – that's what she called it. She detested being tied to the house and the boy. Nappies and shopping – all the usual things that go with running a home.' He scoffed. 'A home! That's the last thing it was. I suppose some of it was my fault – not intentionally, of course. But in my business I was often away from home, abroad very often. It wouldn't have been so bad if she'd been able to come with me sometimes. Not that I could have afforded it, but with Mark it was out of the question. It didn't help when I went to somewhere like New York or Paris, either. She didn't realise that it was all work, with little time for play. Those were the places she wanted to be. The bright lights, that's what she called it. It's all right for you, she would say – always living it up in the bright lights. Huh! If only she'd known. The result was that she became terribly morose.'

'You say she was a model when you met her?'

'Yeah. Didn't you know that?'

42

'No, we didn't. When she died she was a secretary at the Foreign Office.'

Lambert could not disguise his astonishment. 'Ah come off it. You're putting me on?'

'Not at all,' said Tipper.

'Well I'll be damned.' He shook his head and smiled. 'That's incredible.' He laughed. 'That really is something.' He gazed across the room, vacantly, occupied with some introverted reflection. 'Mind you, she was quite bright,' he said. 'Mentally, I mean. She always read *The Times*. Always well up in politics.' He leaned back and stretched his arms across his chest. 'Believe it or not she'd been to a very good school. As a matter of fact she had the chance to go to university, but turned it down, so she said. Too impatient, I suppose. Too impatient for everything. You know she used to get quite moody about having to look after young Mark. She wanted him grown up and off her hands, I think, but didn't want to get old herself, if you know what I mean. She was always worried about her figure, weighing herself – that sort of thing. And she'd get the tape measure out practically every evening, measuring her vital statistics. I'll say that for her – she had a marvellous figure. A marvellous figure and a good brain. She should have had it all going for her, really.' He shook his head and smiled at some distant memory. 'South Woodford – that's where we lived – didn't suit her. In fact she said so – several times, particularly when she was in a mood. "If I'd had any sense," she said once, "I'd have married a stockbroker or an earl, with a Rolls Royce and a Mayfair penthouse." She had this thing about being a lady – a real lady, I mean, married to a lord.' He paused and looked up. 'Stupid bitch,' he said.

'What sort of modelling did she do?' asked Tipper.

Lambert's eyes narrowed slightly. 'The usual. Fashion stuff. The sort you see in magazines and women's papers. Birds with weird hairstyles standing in unnatural poses

43

showing off clothes that real women would never be seen dead in.'

'Who did she work for? Anyone in particular?'

'Yes. Some poof called Darwin – Bob Darwin.'

'You mean he was a homosexual?'

'Oh no. He just looked like one. All the usual gear – shirt undone to the waist, gold neck chain and dyed hair. I always remember that about him – the dyed hair. I hope it's all dropped out. He'd never have been able to cope with baldness. Probably spend a bloody fortune on wigs. He reckoned she had a great future. Mind you, it wouldn't surprise me to learn that she'd been doing a bit of soft porn for him.'

'What makes you think that?'

'Just a feeling – nothing more, but I knew her, don't forget. I must admit I never saw any pictures of her in the porno mags.'

'You read them, do you?'

'No more than anyone else. I'd occasionally flip through one in the hairdressers. There's a big foreign market, of course. If he'd taken any of Penny he could've been knocking them out abroad – Holland or Denmark, or wherever. But, again, I never saw any.'

'You seem to know a lot about the pornographic business, Mr Lambert.'

'No more than I've read in the newspapers – and seen abroad. If you travel a lot – and I do in my trade – you see the bookstalls in places like Amsterdam and Copenhagen overflowing with them.' He laughed. 'It's only the foreigners over there that buy them.'

'When you met her – the Christmas before last – what was she doing then? Did you ask?'

'No idea. Just said "Hallo" and "How are you?" – the usual banal greeting. Frankly I couldn't have cared less how she was.'

'Where did she go when she left you? At least I presume it was she who left you, and not the other way round.'

44

'Oh yes. She went. Left me to sort things out. D'you know I even had to get rid of Mark's clothes. That cut me up, I can tell you. Still does. But I don't think it touched her one bit. It wouldn't have been quite so bad if she had shown any sort of remorse. But nothing; she couldn't have cared less. I kept telling myself that she was hiding it – bottling it all up inside, but on reflection I think she was almost glad.' He hesitated and looked at the carpet. 'Christ she was one hard little bitch.'

'And where did she go?'

'She shacked up with this Darwin bloke. I reckon they deserved each other.'

'This man Darwin – Bob Darwin, I think you said?' Lambert nodded. 'Where was he working then, do you know?'

'Can't remember.' He gave the impression he wasn't going to try very hard. 'Somewhere behind Wardour Street, I think. One of those seedy little studios. Don't recall exactly. There are dozens of them round there. I suppose the material for their porn movies is easier to get in that area.' He was very bitter.

'Did he make porn movies, then?'

Lambert spread his hands. 'Like I said, I could never prove it, but it wouldn't surprise me. I suppose they have to make a crust, and that seems a pretty easy way of doing it. Bloody sight easier than selling computers, I can tell you.' He added the last with a savage laugh.

'Did you ever take any photographs of your wife, Mr Lambert?'

Lambert had been gazing reflectively at the floor and looked up sharply. 'Yes, of course. But I doubt if I've got any now.' He stood up and went into another room.

When he returned he handed Tipper half a dozen snapshots. 'There are these, but they're all of Mark.'

Tipper shuffled quickly through them. One of them had been torn so that only the picture of the small boy remained. He didn't need to ask if the missing half had been a photograph of Penelope Lambert – her ex-husband's attitude had made that fairly obvious, but he asked just the same.

'Yeah! I tore up all the pictures I had of her – straight after I threw her out.'

'You married again now?' asked Tipper.

'Not bloody likely,' said Lambert vehemently. 'Once bitten, as they say.'

Tipper stood up. 'Thanks for your help, Mr Lambert.'

'Aren't you supposed to say something like "We may have to see you again", or "Don't leave town"?'

Tipper smiled. 'I'm sure we'll be able to find you if we need to, Mr Lambert.'

Chapter Four

The telephone call came the second day after Tipper and Markham had seen James Lambert. An ex-policeman working for a cross-Channel ferry company somewhat apologetically rang to say that a grip had been left on their Portsmouth to St Malo service some weeks back and had been placed, as was the custom, in the lost property store at the British port. During a sort out it had been opened and had been found to contain, among other things, a passport in the name of Mrs Penelope Lambert. The grip had been placed in a plastic bag by the Portsmouth scenes-of-crime officer who had then brought it to Scotland Yard – a necessary procedure to preserve the continuity of evidence. The Portsmouth police had been thorough. The officer also brought a bundle of statements proving the link from the delivering officer right back to the deck-hand who had found it, abandoned in one of the luggage bays in the passenger lounge.

The senior fingerprint officer and the liaison officer from the forensic science laboratory came to see Harry Tipper together. They brought the grip and placed it on a side table in his office.

'Fairly common sort of heavy nylon grip, Harry,' said the lab man briskly. 'Obtainable at most outlets. And contained . . . ' He emptied the grip gently onto the table. 'The top half of a well-known bikini . . . ' He pushed a bra towards Tipper with a hand encased in a plastic glove. 'And five pairs of briefs, ditto bras. A sun dress, two ordinary dresses – acrylic, six pairs of tights, pair of shorts, a towelling beachrobe, pair of sandals, pair of court shoes. There's also the usual bits and pieces, like a quantity of cosmetics, a can of hair spray and a hairbrush, a few handkerchiefs, some tissues and finally, a passport and camera.' He picked up the last two items and placed them in front of Tipper.

Tipper pointed to the camera. 'Anything in that?'

'Nope! It's been taken out. I checked with the police at Portsmouth, and they've interviewed everyone who handled the grip. None of them has taken the film. I can only assume that the person or persons unknown took it – and I can think of a very good reason in the circumstances.'

'So can I,' said Tipper. 'Photography seems to be playing a pretty large part in this enquiry.'

'You will doubtless be interested to know,' said the fingerprint officer, 'that we found a half impression on the camera – on the inside. It could have been left by the person who removed the film – it's in the right place. And it's almost certainly identical with one of the sets on the letter of resignation. It'd never go to court because I haven't got sixteen points, but I'd put money on it. Sorry I can't be more helpful.'

'And the passport?'

'No chance. Can't get a single worthwhile print off that.' He smiled ruefully. 'But then you wouldn't expect me to, would you, Harry?'

'Always hope,' said Tipper with a smile.

After the experts had left, Tipper took a pair of plastic gloves out of his desk drawer, and putting them on, poked about among the late Mrs Lambert's belongings. He had no hope of finding anything that had been overlooked; both the laboratory and the fingerprint branch were very thorough.

'Bloody marvellous,' said Markham acidly.

'Two more actions,' said Tipper. 'One – find Darwin. Two – try for a passenger list, or a loading manifest on that cross–Channel ferry for the day this lot was abandoned. I don't think we've got a hope in hell, but we've got to try.'

Markham shrugged. 'We don't even know for certain that it was found on the same day that it was left there, sir.'

'True, Charlie, but you know the rules.'

Markham sighed and left the office to set in train what both he and Tipper believed would be another useless enquiry.

The second action was resolved first, and quickly. The purser was adamant that the grip would have been found at the end of the voyage on which it was abandoned. He regarded as a personal slight the suggestion that the crew would have overlooked it. The ship, he said, was cleaned from stem to stern after every voyage. In any event, said the purser, that particular crewman had started a week's leave that day; so the luggage was definitely handed in on the Monday morning. But the passenger manifest was a different matter. There was now no record and a check with head office produced the same result. The chief clerk plaintively asserted that if they were to keep all the booking forms that long, the office would be buried in paper. Which was a pity, because the grip had been left there during the night crossing which had docked at Portsmouth exactly sixty minutes after Colonel Matthieu had discovered the body of Penelope Lambert.

Charlie Markham was quite disappointed with Bob Darwin's studio. There wasn't a naked woman anywhere to be seen. In fact the only occupant, when they called, was Darwin himself.

'Don't often see the law in here,' he said. 'Leastways, not since the bad old days of the porn squad. Know what I

49

mean?' He winked. 'Well, gents, and what can I do for you? If you're looking for dirty books, I'm afraid you've come to the wrong casino. Straight photographer is Bob Darwin – ask anyone round here.'

'We're investigating a murder, Mr Darwin.' Tipper knew how to sort out the Darwins of this world.

The bravado evaporated. 'Murder? Now just hold on. I don't know anything about a murder. I mean when was this?'

'I understand,' said Tipper, 'that you once employed a Mrs Penelope Lambert?'

'No – at least I can't remember anyone of that name.'

Tipper nodded to Markham who produced a photograph from his pocket. It wasn't the one provided by the gendarmerie, but one which the detectives had found in her flat.

'This woman,' said Tipper.

'That's Penny Gaston – yes, I remember her all right.'

'Gaston? Is that what she called herself?'

'I don't know about "called herself". I only ever knew her as that.'

Tipper made a mental note to run a check at St Catherine's House – the General Register Office – to see if Gaston had been the girl's maiden name. 'When was she working here?' he asked.

'Well on and off from about six or seven years back.'

'By on and off I take it you mean she was a casual rather than a full-time employee?'

Darwin laughed. 'I haven't got any full-time employees here, apart from the cleaner who comes in three times a week. No, Penny was a model. You don't employ them – you just hire 'em when you need them. But she was very good was Penny. She'll go places that girl.'

'Not any more,' said Markham laconically. 'She's dead.'

'Oh my God!' said Darwin. 'Is it her you're talking about?'

50

Tipper nodded. 'I'm afraid so. When did you last see her, Mr Darwin?'

Darwin looked pensive. 'It could only have been a few weeks ago. I'd have to look at my diary, but I think she was in about the beginning of August. I'd got a nail-varnish job to do, bit swift. Very good hands Penny'd got – apart from everything else, of course.' He gave a lascivious leer.

'Did she ever work for any other photographers, d'you know?'

Darwin laughed. 'You'd better believe it. With a figure like she'd got, they were falling over each other.'

Tipper decided it was time to knock this popinjay over. 'How long did she live with you, Mr Darwin?'

'Bloody hell,' said Darwin. 'You don't pull any punches, do you?'

'Well?'

Darwin considered the question. 'For about six months – it was a good six months,' he said reflectively. 'Then I threw her out.' He added the last apprehensively. The police might be thinking that he had had something to do with her death.

'Why?'

'I found she was having it off with some other photographer.' He spread his hands. 'I didn't really mind that – I'm very broad-minded, but I was bloody well keeping her. So I told her to make up her mind. And she did, the cow – she went.'

'Name?'

'Now look, fellahs . . . '

'Name?' asked Tipper again.

Darwin paused, reluctant. 'Charley Godley,' he said.

'Address?'

'Wardour Court. It's not far from here – up towards Berners Street.'

'I know where it is, Mr Darwin. How long ago did she go?'

Darwin scratched at his dyed hair – Markham noted that it was all still there. ''Bout four years ago. Mind you, I've seen her from time to time since, like I said. She did quite a few jobs for me. She was very good.'

'So we've been hearing,' said Markham.

'She was a great girl to have about the place. Full of fun. We lived upstairs here.' He pointed towards the ceiling. 'There was no holding her when she got going. Organise a party at the drop of a hat. If she'd had a good week – you know, plenty of sessions, she'd come in with a couple of bottles of champagne. I'd have to match them and we'd have a private party. Christ, she was a wild one. But dangerous. She kept trying to talk me into the porn business. Offered to do poses for me – quite uninhibited, she was. But I'm not into that.'

Markham gave him a cynical look.

'No really,' he said. 'It's too bloody risky these days. Your blokes from West End Central would be down here like a shot. It's just not worth it.'

'Did she mention her husband at all?' asked Tipper.

'Husband? When did she get married then?'

'Before she came to live with you, Mr Darwin.'

'Get off. Really?' Tipper nodded. 'She never mentioned being married, not once. Are you sure?'

'Very,' said Tipper.

'Well the saucy little cow. Mind you, nothing 'd surprise me about her. You never knew what she was going to get up to next. I was better off when she went, to be quite honest. She frightened me at times. D'you know she came down here one afternoon when I'd got a session going, just wearing a bottle of champagne and nothing else. Smashed, she was – absolutely smashed. Gave me a right bollocking for not joining her party and then collapsed on the floor – out cold.'

'Upset your customers did it?'

'Not really, no. I'd only got one queer doing men's under-wear. Didn't bat an eyelid – well he wouldn't would he? Still they're used to it round here. Happens all the time.'

'Would you be prepared to let us have a set of your fingerprints, for elimination purposes, Mr Darwin?'

He looked doubtful. 'What's that for, then?'

'You don't have to, of course. But it makes it easier for us to reduce the field of suspects – by taking out the innocent marks. It leaves us with just one set – we hope.'

'Yes. All right.' But he still sounded reluctant.

'Charley Godley, you say?'

'That's right,' said Darwin, and laughed.

'I'll bet we've got his dabs on file already,' said Markham, once they were back in the street.

'Racing certainty, I should think,' said Tipper.

The front door was open, and Tipper and Markham mounted the uncarpeted wooden staircase. The large front room of what, years ago, had been a fashionable town house, was the photographer's studio; lights, tripods, a few papier mâché Grecian columns, and the other paraphernalia of the trade, gave an impression of utter chaos.

On a podium at one end of the room stood an effeminate young man, striking an unnatural pose, and displaying a bottle of aftershave lotion.

The photographer, busily moving about and taking shot after shot with a hand-held camera, was a woman. Tipper estimated that she was about forty years old. She was wearing a pair of faded jeans and a man's shirt outside them. Her long grey hair was worn in a single pigtail that reached almost to her waist, braided very tightly off the face to reveal sharply sculpted but not unattractive features.

She glanced briefly at the two policemen and carried on with her work. 'Be with you shortly, loves,' she said over her shoulder. A few minutes later she put her camera down and stretched her arms above her head. 'That'll do, Jason. Thank you, love.'

The young man stepped down to the floor and donned a leather jacket. The photographer opened a cash-box, counted out some bank notes and gave them to her model. 'See you, love,' she said, and waited until his footsteps had receded down the stairs before turning to the two detectives.

'Now dears, what can I do for you?' She studied their faces in turn, carefully, as if appraising their photogenic qualities.

'We're police officers,' said Tipper.

The woman nodded. 'I thought so.'

'We're looking for Mr Godley.'

The woman threw back her head and laughed. 'You and me both,' she said. 'I haven't seen the bastard in years.' Her voice was well modulated and attractive, the accent that of an educated woman; the language she used sounded strange in those tones.

'Mr Charles Godley – Charley Godley.'

'Uh uh!' She shook her head. 'Tony was his name. I'm Charley – short for Charlotte.' She smiled. 'Thanks to my father who was a great lover of the Brontë sisters. Not physically of course.' She paused, and laughed again.

Tipper wanted to get it right. 'You're Charley Godley?'

'S'right!' She smiled once more. 'Well everybody's got to be somebody.'

'Did you know a Mrs Penelope Lambert?'

'Yes, I did. She wasn't known as that, though. Always called herself Penny Gaston, but yes, I did know her. Why?'

Tipper ignored the question. 'Did she live here at one time?'

'Not here. This is my workshop. No, she lived with me at my house at Richmond.' She thrust her hands into the pockets of her jeans. 'We had a lesbian relationship.' She looked Tipper straight in the eyes with an unwavering stare.

'I see.' Tipper realised now why Darwin had laughed.

'I doubt if you do,' she said. 'Men don't usually. They're so damned chauvinistic that it hurts their ego to think that

54

a woman can be attracted by another woman and be quite satisfied with that.'

'Who was Tony then?'

'My husband.'

'Oh!'

'And no, he didn't leave me because I was a lesbian, because I wasn't then. Anyway, what is this – an enquiry into my private life, or are you really a television crew doing a fly-on-the-wall programme?'

'No – it's an enquiry into Penelope Lambert's private life. When did you last see her, Mrs Godley?'

She didn't answer immediately, but walked across to a table and poured half a tumbler of Scotch. She turned, holding the bottle in the air, a questioning expression on her face.

'No thank you,' said Tipper. Markham said nothing.

She took a mouthful of the neat spirit and walked back to the detectives, still holding the glass. 'Eight or nine weeks ago – something like that. Why what's she done?'

'Got herself murdered, Mrs Godley.'

Charley Godley's expression did not change. 'I can't say I'm surprised,' she said, without emotion. 'Can't say I'm surprised at all.'

'Why is that?'

'She played the field did Penny. Always got some man in tow – but never for long.'

'You mean she was a prostitute?'

'Not in so many words, love, no. But she was – what's that lovely computer expression – user-friendly?'

'How long was she living with you, Mrs Godley?'

'Call me Charley, love – everybody does.' She hesitated, pouting. 'About a year, I suppose.'

'And then?'

'She left.' Charley Godley shrugged at life's inevitabilities. 'Went to live with a fellah. She's what round here they

55

call ambidextrous. Quite inappropriate use of the term, of course.'

'But you continued to see her from time to time?'

'Oh yes. We didn't part bad friends. It just seemed better that we didn't live together any more.'

'When did you first get to know her?'

'A good four years ago, I should think. She just waltzed in one day. Mind you a lot of girls do that – mainly from out of town, from the sticks. Come to London thinking their fanny's their fortune, but find out too late that it's not. I could see that she'd got that sparkle – you pick it up very quickly in this business if you're going to survive – that something that comes through the camera and out the other side. Well in she came and said she was looking for work. Funnily enough I'd just got a job to do for a shower company— '

'Shower company?' Tipper interrupted.

'Yes, love. Firm that makes showers. You know, you stand under 'em and get wet – and clean.'

Tipper smiled. 'Yes of course. Go on.'

'Well girls willing to do a nude pose aren't as easy to find as you might think – not when they're going to be spread all over the newspapers and the rest, but she didn't hesitate. Mind you hunger does some strange things. Anyway, I put it to her and she agreed.'

Suddenly aware that she and the policemen were all still standing Charley sat down on a chair and smiled. 'I'm sorry,' she said, 'keeping you standing. Do sit down. The furniture's not up to much, but I don't usually entertain here.'

Tipper and Markham pulled up a couple of cane chairs – chairs which had seen better days – and sat down facing the woman.

'Apparently,' said Charley, when she was settled, 'she'd just had the mother and father of all rows with her bloke. Apparently he'd put it to her that she ought to do some

56

porn movies. Well, she said she didn't mind doing some skin stuff – that's what we call the nude poses in the trade – but she drew the line at the porno. She said he was always on about it and it was beginning to get on her nerves . . . '

'Did she say who this man was?'

'Yes. Bob somebody. I can't remember now.'

'Darwin?'

'That's it – Bob Darwin. Anyway she'd decided to move out – leave him. But there was one problem – she hadn't got anywhere to go. I took pity on her and said that she could have a room in my place down at Richmond. She jumped at it. Was back to this Darwin bloke the same afternoon and packed her things, and in she came.'

'And did she continue to work for you?'

'Yes, of course, but not exclusively, if that's what you mean. There was nothing written into the tenancy. She just carried on as before – getting work where she could. None of us in this business can afford to pay a model a wage – even if you're one of the top names, and I'm not. There'd be no point. You can't use one model for everything. No, the accommodation was a separate arrangement. But it's very small. We tended to live on top of each other. She used to roam about with nothing on, quite unabashed. To be perfectly honest, I never thought I'd get into that sort of thing— ' She broke off, for the first time looking a little embarrassed. 'And, frankly, I don't think she did, either – it just happened. She'd had this terrible trauma, with her little boy – you know about that, I suppose?' Tipper nodded. 'And she was clearly still cut up about it, although it was getting on for a year. I think she missed having a family – you know, husband and a kiddy to care for. I suppose it was the older woman thing – a mother figure. Sometimes she would sit down and pour her heart out. Poor little bitch. Apparently her husband was an absolute swine. And then she jumped out of the frying pan into the fire. This Bob Darwin character was no better – well that's men all over,

57

isn't it? The upshot was that we both suddenly realised –
at about the same time really – that we'd stumbled on a
relationship, her and me, that was uncomplicated by men.
I wouldn't go so far as to say that we were in love. What's
that, after all? But we found that we were compatible. As
for sex – well, when you've been married . . . I don't have
to say any more, not to blokes like you, do I?'

She stood up and walked over to the table where the
whisky was and poured herself another half-tumbler. 'Are
you sure you won't have one?' she asked.

'Quite sure,' said Tipper.

'But it was too good to last, our little love-nest. She was
always restless – always seeking the unattainable, I think.
Anyway she came in one day – right out of the blue – and
said that she'd met this wonderful bloke, and that was it.'

'And she went?'

'Oh yes. She went.'

'Who was he – any idea?'

'A civil servant, apparently. Some wonderful, steady
bloke, just what she'd always been looking for. And this
was it. Love and happiness at last. I don't think it was,
though. Well I know it wasn't, because I saw her from
time to time afterwards. It was the usual story. The great
dream, and then it started to fragment, the way it always
does – and I should know. She tried to pretend it was all
hunky-dory, but you can tell. I know jolly well it wasn't.
There are giveaway signs.'

'What was the name of this bloke she went to live with
– or did she marry him?'

'He was called John something – I'm afraid I can't help
you more than that. But no – she didn't marry him. She
said it was on trial to start with. She'd had one marriage
that had gone horribly wrong, and she was going to make
sure before she committed herself again. As I say, she still
worked for me, whenever I'd got anything. I'm afraid that's
all I can tell you about her. But it doesn't surprise me that

she was murdered. She was a nice girl, but overwhelming, if you know what I mean. She would really go overboard – and men don't like that – it frightens the hell out of them.'

'And you last saw her eight weeks ago?'

'Eight or nine, yes. She popped in, looking for work, as usual.'

'And had you got any for her?'

'Not any more, love, no. It was funny really, after all she had had to say about porn. But she offered to do some calendar work – you know, the *risqué* stuff?' She raised an eyebrow. The two policemen nodded. They knew what she meant. 'But I couldn't help her. I don't do that sort of thing. But she'd found out that it paid better – a hell of a lot better.' She caught Markham's cynical look. 'I don't mix business with pleasure,' she said and laughed.

'He was a civil servant, you say – this bloke she went to live with?'

'So she said.'

Just as they had reached a 'J' that could have been the 'J' in the diary, they were frustrated again. Of course you didn't have to be a professional to take photographs of a girl. 'Have you any idea where he lived, this civil servant?'

'No, I'm sorry – no idea. Civil servants tend to keep their addresses secret, if they're in this area; they're usually up to something naughty. The girls round here could tell some tales that would make your hair stand on end.' She reflected on that for a moment. 'Probably not you two,' she said. 'Coppers know all about that sort of thing, don't they?'

'I wonder if we could bother you to provide us with a set of what we call elimination fingerprints, Mrs Godley. It's a system whereby we try to eradicate all the innocent prints from the ones we've got, so that, hopefully, we finish up with the murderer.'

'Of course. I've done it before, actually.' The word sounded upper class. 'But I've got another session in about five minutes time. Could we make it around six-thirty? I might even let you buy me a drink afterwards.'

'Yes, of course. I'll get Detective Sergeant Markham here to pick you up in a car and run you round to West End Central. It'll not take too long. All right, Charlie?'

'Yes,' she said.

'No, not you – him,' said Tipper. 'He's called Charlie, too.'

'Well there's a thing,' said Charley Godley.

Markham looked at this curiously attractive lesbian and wondered if she too was still ambidextrous.

Chapter Five

The great detective, working alone, and possessed of some sixth sense which enables him to identify the author of a crime, without recourse to the evidence, is a creation of the fiction writer. There is no place for such an individual in the incident room which is the centre of any investigation into a major crime.

The setting up of an incident room is a matter which needs great attention. The experienced senior officer will select very carefully the sergeant he puts in charge of it, because it is upon the skill of that individual that the investigation succeeds or founders. The Incident Room Sergeant is a combination of many things. He will be a seasoned investigator who has played a part in many serious crime enquiries. And he will be a proven administrator, capable of producing order out of chaos, and supporting the detectives in the field. He will know the right people to contact when he needs something in a hurry. He will charm stationery out of reluctant storekeepers, and have telephone lines installed from an exchange with no spare lines. He will persuade officers much senior to him to part with additional detectives which they not only cannot spare but didn't even know they had.

One of the members of the team is a statement-reader. His task is to read every statement which has been taken, always on the date it is taken, and mark up aspects which need to be further investigated. The senior officer in charge will do the same, and will often mark up things which the statement-reader has missed or which, for him, have no apparent significance. It is true that these days the computer will play a big part in assisting a complicated enquiry, but it will never be a substitute for the human element.

When a further enquiry is identified in this way it is entered in the action book, and given a number. The sergeant in charge of the incident room then allocates it to a detective to pursue. The result, often in the form of another statement, will be analysed, and may cause further 'actions' to be initiated. It is all very tedious and mundane, and has none of the excitement that television writers would have you believe is the daily round of the detective.

One such action, allocated to a junior detective constable on the Lambert job, was a thorough examination of Mrs Lambert's diary and address book. Everybody has one or the other – or both. And everybody is prone to jot down telephone numbers with a brief reference, often just a Christian name. And so it was with Penelope Lambert. Each of the telephone numbers in her diary was passed to British Telecom, and the subscriber traced. Each one has to be checked in this way because policemen have found, over the years, that the human being is a devious creature. The telephone number with the name of a man against it in a man's diary will be found to be that of the girl-friend that he doesn't want his wife to know about; or a work colleague's name will have a bookmaker's telephone number alongside it, and so on.

Most of the telephone numbers in Mrs Lambert's book turned out to be innocuous: the hairdresser, her doctor, the garage – she was always having trouble with her car, and various other people and firms who have to be rung up from time to time. But there were one or two that were not immediately significant.

'Put an action in the book to trace this civil servant John, will you, Charlie,' said Tipper.

'Done it, guv, for what good it will do,' said Markham.

'Mustn't be downhearted.'

'Well, blimey, guv'nor. I read somewhere that there are a million civil servants in this country; on a conservative estimate, I reckon two-thirds of them must be men. And how many d'you think are called John?'

'A lot,' said Tipper, unhelpfully.

It was easier than it seemed. 'That address book,' said the Incident Room Sergeant. 'Who was doing that?'

'Fred Logan, skip,' said someone.

'Fetch him here,' said the Sergeant.

'Any civil servants in that book of hers, Fred?' asked the Sergeant.

'Yes,' said Logan. 'At least – could be.'

'Spit it out, lad.'

'There's a number here, with an extension, that goes out to the Department of Trade. It's got "John" written beside it.'

'And?'

'That's all.'

'Well who's John?'

'Dunno, skip.'

'Well bloody well find out – that's what you're paid for.'

A chastened Detective Constable Logan made enquiries of the security officer at the Department of Trade and Industry, and was told that no one called 'John' was on that extension. However, said the security officer, there had been up until six months ago. A principal called John Wallace who lived in Surbiton.

'Charley Godley, guv.'

'What about her?' Tipper was slumped in his office chair, balancing a pencil between his two forefingers, and trying

63

to line it up with the bottom of the group photograph of his advanced CID course at Hendon which hung on the opposite wall.

'I'm not happy about her, sir.'

'Refuse your advances, did she?'

'Didn't make any, thank you very much,' said Markham with a sniff.

'Well then?'

'Lesbians can be very spiteful when someone upsets them.'

'Oh do get on, Charlie. What are you saying?'

'I'm saying,' said Markham patiently, 'that it wouldn't surprise me to find that she murdered Penny Lambert – out of sheer bloody jealousy.'

'Oh!' said Tipper, still playing with his pencil, 'And what, apart from illogical intuition, leads you to that astounding proposition?'

'She was away the same time as Penelope was.'

Tipper slowly sat up. 'How do you know that?'

'I checked with the keyholders' register at West End Central, and there was a cross-reference to the unattended premises cards. Her studio at Wardour Court was unattended for the week.'

'And?'

'And nothing, sir. That's as far as I've got.'

Tipper stood up and turned to the window. He parted the slats and gazed down into Broadway. It was a habit of his; he wasn't looking for anything. 'There's a berk down there just parked his van across the exit to the Yard car-park,' he said. 'I just hope for his sake that the first car up isn't a Flying Squad one – his feet won't touch.' He turned back. 'Well I think, in that case, that a few discreet enquiries won't come amiss, Charlie.'

'It's in hand, guv. I've put it out as an action.'

'Well get it back again. I don't want some idiot DC

64

trying to tie Charley Godley up in knots, because he won't succeed – she's far too astute.' He sat down again and swivelled his chair gently from side to side. 'Come to think of it, Charlie, her answers were much too pat. She wasn't at all surprised when we told her that Penny'd been murdered – in fact, she said as much. I would have thought that she would have shown some emotion. After all, she did have a – what was that expression of hers?'

'A relationship,' said Markham, flipping through the pages of his pocket-book.

'Yes . . . ' Tipper spoke thoughtfully. 'And it lasted a year – that's what she claimed, wasn't it?'

'Yes. "About a year, I suppose," is what she said.' Again Markham quoted from his notes.

'Interesting. Here we have a woman who has a lesbian affair with the victim which lasts a year, and then . . . ' He broke off. 'How long was it since she had last seen her, Charlie?'

'Eight or nine weeks, sir.'

'Yeah! Then the Old Bill turns up and tells her that her ex-girlfriend has been murdered, and she doesn't even ask what happened. She wasn't interested in how, or where; she didn't ask a single question about the circumstances. Now what d'you make of that?'

'Some people are very private,' said Markham.

'Philosopher now, are you?' Tipper said, an edge of sarcasm in his voice.

'No, it's just that she might have waited before crying her bloody eyes out. You know what some people are like.'

'Yes, you could be right, and she's the sort of woman who may never display any emotion. P'raps that's why her old man left her,' he added as an aside. 'But there's a limit. If someone tells you, out of the blue, that someone you've lived with for a year has been murdered, and that's

65

the first you know of it, it's very difficult to hide some surprise, isn't it?'

'You may have put your finger on it, guv.' Tipper raised a quizzical eyebrow. 'Well,' continued Markham, 'you said, "if that's the first you know of it". Maybe it wasn't.' The Sergeant paused again.

'There again,' said Tipper, 'Perhaps lesbians are different.'

Markham smirked. 'I don't think there's much argument about that,' he said.

'I know a bit more about queers,' said Tipper, as if Markham hadn't spoken. 'But I have to admit that lesbians are a bit of a mystery to me.' He stood up. 'Take that one on yourself, Charlie. See what you can find out, and then perhaps we'll go and have another little chat with Muzz Charley Godley.'

Detective Sergeant Markham found out nothing beyond confirming, from what the police euphemistically call local enquiries, that Charley Godley's Wardour Court studio had been locked up, and apparently unattended during the week that culminated with the death of Penelope Lambert. Other people in the immediate vicinity knew her, obviously, but had no idea where she had been during those seven days. One conscientious beat-duty PC recalled having checked the premises on a couple of nights, and that without incident. A similar enquiry of Richmond police station produced the same story. Charley Godley's house in Richmond had been registered as unattended, but no one locally knew where she had gone. A neighbour had stood in as keyholder, but understood that Mrs Godley, whom she knew only slightly, was away – touring, she thought. It left but one alternative.

'We'll have to go and see her again, Charlie,' said Tipper.

They paused at the bottom of the stairs leading to Charley's first-floor studio to allow an attractive girl to come down. She smiled sweetly at Markham and thanked Tipper as she went out to the street.

'D'you think I should have warned that young lady that she was in moral danger?' asked Markham.

'So might you be,' said Tipper acidly.

'Oh, it's you,' said Charley Godley, emerging from an inner doorway and wiping her hands on a towel. 'Sit down. I'm just making a cup of tea, if you're interested?'

'Thanks, yes,' said Tipper.

After a few minutes the photographer reappeared with a tray on which were three large chipped mugs. 'Help yourself to sugar,' she said, and sat down facing them. 'Well?' She gazed levelly at the two policemen.

Tipper decided that there was no point in prevaricating with this woman, 'You were away from here, and indeed from your address in Richmond, between the sixteenth and the twenty-fifth of August.'

Charley Godley said nothing, but stood up and walked to a table on the other side of the room. It was covered with papers and obviously was used as a desk. She thumbed through a large scribbling diary that lay in the centre of the jumble until she found the right entry. With her back to the detectives she said: 'Correct. Actually it was the fifteenth as well – the Friday.' She closed the book with a slam and turned to face them. 'Why?'

'Where did you go, Mrs Godley?'

'Well, if it's any of your business, loves, France.'

Tipper was not pleased with her reply. She was either supremely confident – or innocent.

'Whereabouts in France?'

'The south. Cannes – well, just outside. Why are you asking these questions?'

'Did you go alone, or was there someone with you, Mrs Godley?'

'No I was not alone – I was with someone.'

'Who?'

'I'm not answering any more of your questions until you tell me why you want to know these things.' She was quite cool, unruffled by the Chief Inspector's probing.

'Because,' said Tipper, 'during the week you were away, Penny Lambert was murdered – in France.'

Charley Godley smiled, stood up and walked over to the side-table where she kept the whisky. 'You boys going to join me in one?' she asked.

'No, thank you.'

She walked back to her chair and sat down. 'You don't honestly think that I murdered that little tramp, do you?'

'You seemed more compassionate than that, last time we spoke to you about her,' said Tipper.

She stared into her whisky as if trying to see something beyond the amber liquid, seeking, almost, a vision, as a fortune-teller will search a crystal ball.

'Well I'm a bit old-fashioned,' she said. 'My father always brought us kids up never to blacken the dead.' She smiled and shook her head, recalling the father who was obsessed with the Brontë sisters. She looked up at Tipper. 'She was an absolute cow. We had one blazing row after another. Oh, sure, we had a relationship, but Christ, what a tempestuous relationship it was. Just like husband and wife, really.' She interrupted herself: 'I suppose that it's difficult for you – for any man – to understand that sort of thing. But I loved that damned girl – really loved her, more than I ever loved my husband – or any other man, for that matter. And I got nothing in return. She was a bitch. She would go out with men, and taunt me with them afterwards, making comparisons.' Suddenly, and quite uncharacteristically, she started crying, holding her head in her hands and trying to hide her distress. Just as quickly she stopped, and looked up, dabbing her eyes with a tissue she had taken from her jeans pocket. 'I'm sorry, loves, that's not the real me.' She shook her head, as if clearing her mind of unpleasant memories. 'The rest is true; after the final row she pushed off to live with this bloody civil servant of hers – John.' She put the tissue back in her pocket and braced herself – almost a shake. 'I'm sorry. No. I didn't kill her. I must admit that I felt like it on more than one occasion, but I loved her too much.' She stopped again. 'I suppose I always thought that she might come back, that I might persuade her . . . '

Tipper was a cynic, the result of too many such interviews, and dealing with too many criminals, who would produce Oscar-like performances to preserve their liberty. When the chips were down, he always thought, it concentrated the mind wonderfully.

'Thank you, Mrs Godley,' he said. 'We've interrupted your work for long enough. Perhaps we can come back and see you again?' When we've got a little more evidence to screw you with, he thought.

'Oh, don't let that worry you,' she said. 'I've had nothing to do all afternoon.'

Tipper thought of the girl they had met on the stairs, and willed Markham to say nothing.

'Guess where we're going now?' said Tipper when they reached the street.

'Richmond, at a rough guess, guv'nor.'

That Charley Godley was as shrewd as they had given her credit for was borne out by the fact that the pretty girl they had met on the stairs of her studio wasn't in the least surprised to find two policemen on the doorstep of Charley Godley's house.

'I didn't expect to see you again so soon,' she said, holding the door open. 'You'd better come in.'

The trained eyes of the detectives assessed the girl as she settled herself confidently in an armchair. About twenty-eight, they reckoned – Penny's age. She had long blonde hair, and wore tight jeans with boots, and a loose scarlet blouse, tied at the low neckline with a black ribbon. She wore a plain gold wedding ring, but who had given it to her was a matter of speculation.

'Charley told me to expect you,' she said.

'Oh?'

'She rang me, just after you left the studio. Why are you harassing her?'

'We're not. We're making enquiries into a serious offence.'

She smiled tolerantly. 'I suppose you want to ask me if I went on holiday with Charley in the south of France in August?'

'No,' said Tipper. 'I want to ask you when you went?'

'On Friday the fifteenth. We caught the morning plane from Heathrow – nine fifty-five, it was, on Air France. Arrived at Nice at about a quarter to one; very civilised. Anything else you want to know?'

'Yes. Where did you go from there?'

'We got a taxi out to Cannes.'

'Yes?' Tipper raised his eyebrows.

'We had hired a villa – just outside Cannes, actually,' she said. 'Idyllic. Swimming pool – everything.'

'Sounds expensive.'

'It was.'

'There must be more money in photography than I thought,' said Tipper.

'I paid for it, if you must know,' said the girl. She sat gazing at the detectives in a very cool, relaxed way. 'And to save you asking your cat-and-mouse questions, Charley and I have a lesbian relationship – which should come as no surprise to you. And since you haven't yet asked, but will do so, sooner or later, my name is Sheila Johnson, and I'm twenty-seven.' She was playing with them now, with a bravado that, in their experience, could only be the result of confidence in her own and Charley's innocence. 'And since you can't take your eyes off this . . .' She extended her left hand to display the ring on her

70

third finger. 'It was given to me by Charley. I'm not married, at least not in the conventional sense, but it suits me – and her. Now, is there anything else? Or are we getting to the stage where I ought to be ringing my solicitor?'

It was an implied threat, but Tipper was accustomed to such hazards in his job. 'Did you stay at Cannes for the whole week?'

'Yes. In fact we stayed in the villa for practically the whole time. I think we went out for a meal about three times. Most of the time we spent in and around the pool.' She smiled – the first injection of humour she had permitted to enter the conversation. 'In fact, we were half drunk for most of the week.'

'Did you go to Brittany at all during that week?'

'Good God, no. That's miles away. Why?'

'Because that's where the murdered body of Mrs Godley's last lesbian companion was found, during the same week that you and she were in France, Miss Johnson, that's why.' It was an unnecessarily brutal way of putting it, but Tipper felt inclined to jar this girl's composure.

It had its effect. She paled quite visibly, and her hand went to her mouth. 'My God!' she said, 'I didn't know anything about that. Charley didn't say anything about anyone being murdered. That's terrible.' Perhaps she suddenly felt vulnerable.

'I take it you knew nothing about her previous relationship?'

The girl paused. 'No. No, I didn't.' She looked up truculently. 'So what? It's a free world, and we're all free agents in it. Aren't we?'

'Up to a point, yes,' said Tipper with a smile. 'Have you ever heard of Penelope Lambert – or Penny Gaston, as she was sometimes known?'

Sheila Johnson did not hesitate. 'No, I haven't. Why? Was she Charley's girlfriend?'

71

'Yes. When did your relationship with Mrs Godley begin?' Tipper was taking advantage of the girl's perplexity over the news that they were investigating a murder, asking a few important questions before she recovered her self-confidence.

She thought about that for a moment or two. 'About four months ago, I suppose.'

'What do you do for a living, Miss Johnson?'

'Now?' It was a strange question.

'Yes – now.'

'Nothing. I'm what you would call "of independent means", I suppose.'

'That sounds as if you haven't always been so?'

She uncrossed her legs, and recrossed them the other way. Tipper noticed that her boots were of very good quality – handmade in all probability.

'No,' she said. 'I used to be an escort. I suppose you'd call it being a prostitute.'

It was a feature of whores that Tipper had noticed over the years; they were never reticent about their occupation when talking to policemen and the Inland Revenue – the former usually laughed and the latter were embarrassed.

Tipper laughed. 'And does Charley Godley know what you did for a living?'

The girl smiled a tight smile. 'Of course she does. There are no secrets in Soho, you know.'

'And you're sure you never met Penelope Lambert?'

'I said I'd never heard of her.' She spoke impatiently.

'Why did you stop being a prostitute?'

'Quite simply because I'd made enough money at it. And, contrary to popular opinion, there's not a great deal of job satisfaction in it.'

Markham sniggered, and was rewarded with a withering look from the girl.

'What's more,' she continued, 'you see the worst possible side of men. They're animals. Quite frankly, I'm pissed off with men, which is probably why I became a lesbian – if you're interested.'

'Thank you for your time, Miss Johnson,' said Tipper, standing up.

'Not at all,' she said. 'Just think yourself lucky I'm not still in the trade – it would have cost you about a hundred quid.' There was no humour in the remark, and no one smiled.

'Did you ever take any photographs?' asked Markham, thinking that here was another 'J', and remembering the 'J took photographs' entry in Penny's diary.

She looked at him as if doubting his reason. 'Of course. Hasn't everyone?'

'I meant professionally?'

'I'm not into blackmail,' she said.

'I didn't mean that either,' said Markham, regretting that he had asked the question at all.

'What did you mean then?' She stood, legs apart, hands on hips, defiant.

'I meant were you ever a professional photographer?'

'No. Charley's the photographer. I did a few lewd poses for her – that's how we met.'

'Well I'm damned,' said Markham, as they settled in the car outside Charley Godley's little house. 'After all she said about not being into porn.'

Tipper laughed. 'Wake up, Charlie. It's an easy way to make money, and there's very little risk, because blokes like you and me can never see it as being awfully serious. Who gets harmed by it? There are one or two born-again Christians in the job who get terribly animated about it, but generally speaking they stay in the uniform branch.'

'What d'you think, guv? About Charley Godley, I mean?'

'Bloody waste of time, Charlie. But we'll get our friend Captain Courbet to have a few enquiries made in Cannes, just to see if their story holds up. Otherwise, I think we can forget it.'

73

Chapter Six

John Wallace, the civil servant whose telephone number was in Penny's diary, was mystified to get a call from Scotland Yard, and not a little concerned to learn that two detectives wished to interview him about a matter that they were not prepared to discuss on the phone. They weren't prepared to discuss it because they were by no means certain that John Wallace, albeit a civil servant, was the man that Penelope Lambert had gone to live with when she left Charley Godley. On the face of it a semi in Surbiton did not seem to be the place that might appeal to a girl of the complex character that was now emerging.

It was a three-up-two-down, stucco and pebble-dashed house typical of the thirties era in which it had been built.

Wallace was tall and well-built; if anything a little overweight, with wavy greying hair and the fleshy good looks that often attracted vacuous women and sports-car salesmen alike. Tipper thought that he was about thirty-seven, probably still played rugby, squash and tennis, and talked loudly in pubs, where judging by his complexion, he spent a lot of his time and much of his money.

'This is my wife Linda,' said Wallace, showing them into the sitting room. A tall thin woman with dyed blonde hair and hard features was switching off the television. She did not look particularly pleased to see them.

'Perhaps it might be better if we spoke to you on your own,' said Tipper.

Wallace frowned. 'Anything you want to say, you can say in front of my wife.' He spoke with a certain haughtiness, like a man who believed the myth that an Englishman's home is his castle.

Tipper shrugged. 'As you wish. Does the name Penelope Lambert, or Penny Gaston as she was sometimes known, mean anything to you?'

Linda Wallace gave a short cynical laugh. 'I told you that woman would mean trouble eventually,' she said.

'You knew her?' Tipper looked at Wallace's wife.

'Good Lord no, but John told me all about her. It was before we were married. He lived with her.' She glanced at her husband – a glance which implied that all men were children at heart, and that women knew it.

'Why d'you say that she'd be trouble?'

Linda Wallace's face became serious. 'Aren't all easy women trouble in the long run? She was a model, so she told John, but quite frankly, in my experience, the term model covers a multitude of sins – and I do mean sins.'

'She wasn't like that.' Wallace himself butted in, and Tipper thought that perhaps he had started what policemen call a husband-and-wife dispute.

But Mrs Wallace was contemptuous. 'Come off it,' she said. 'She was available and you fell for it. It wasn't until she found out that you were a civil servant with no money – just debts – that she was happy to let go.' She paused, suspiciously. 'At least, John Wallace,' she said, 'that's what you told me.'

'What's happened exactly?' asked Wallace. 'Has she been arrested or something?'

'Would it surprise you if she had?' asked Tipper quietly.

75

'Well – I don't know exactly. . . . I just wondered why you'd come down to see me about her.'

'She's been murdered.'

'Good God!' said Wallace.

His wife was less sympathetic. 'Well it won't be anything to do with him,' she said, indicating her husband. 'He can't even bring himself to carve the turkey at Christmas.'

Tipper discounted that. In his twenty-two years' service he had met quite a few mild-mannered men who had been convicted of murder. 'When did you start living with her, Mr Wallace?' There was a sudden edge to his voice; he was already tiring of Linda Wallace.

'It must have been about three years ago.' He paused and looked at his wife. 'We've been married, what – two years?'

'Yes, darling.' She spoke sarcastically, in tones that implied that he would undoubtedly forget their anniversary, too.

'How did you meet her?'

'At a party. I had one or two racy friends – I was living in a flat in Battersea at the time – we used to throw these wild parties – couldn't afford them, of course. I can't remember who invited her, but I saw her and thought, yes, I think I'll have some of that . . . '

'And I suppose that's what you thought when you first saw me?' His wife interrupted again.

Wallace ignored her and went on, 'We got talking, and – well, it was all rather quick . . . '

'I'll bet it was,' said Linda Wallace.

'Do you mind.' Wallace snapped sharply at his wife. 'We both agreed that we'd clicked,' he said, turning to Tipper again, 'and she moved into my flat.'

'Where from?' Markham was sitting at the table, making notes.

'D'you know, I haven't the faintest notion. I had this idea at the back of my mind that she lived somewhere locally, sort of Chelsea-ish, but I wasn't sure. Anyway, she moved in – and we lived together for about six months.'

It all sounded just a little too pat for Tipper's liking. 'Just like that?'

Wallace smiled – a little too confidently. 'Yes.'

'Let me get this right,' said Tipper. 'She turned up at one of your parties. You don't know where she came from but after a short conversation you offered her accommodation in your flat, and she moved in? Just like that? No questions – no doubts – no hang-ups. You said "How d'you fancy living with me?", and she agreed. Have I got that right?'

Wallace shrugged and crossed his legs. 'Some people do have all the luck, don't they?' He smiled.

'Who was she living with before, Mr Wallace?'

'I don't know . . . '

'Are you saying that for the whole time she was living with you, she never once mentioned anything about her previous life?'

Wallace looked slightly uncomfortable, and Tipper knew that there was more in this apparently innocent relationship than the man was prepared to reveal. It might simply be the presence of his forbidding wife, with her sarcasm and disdain; on the other hand there might be something very much deeper.

'No, not really. I suppose she made some allusions to it, but I wasn't much interested in what she'd been doing before.'

'And then you met your wife?' Tipper glanced at Linda Wallace, leaning back in her chair, coldly observing her husband as he wriggled.

'Yes.'

'And?'

'Well, I left Penny – in the Battersea flat – and moved down here. The flat was rented, you see, but this was

Linda's house. Linda was divorced. We'd met in the office, and so I—'

'I don't think the gentleman's interested in our affairs, John,' said his wife sharply.

'Did you ever take any photographs of Mrs Lambert?'

Wallace half smiled and appeared to give the matter some careful thought. 'No,' he said, 'no, I don't think I did. Why do you ask? The best I can do is give you a description of her, but—'

'We know what she looks like, Mr Wallace. Incidentally, when did you last see her?'

Wallace didn't hesitate. 'The day I moved out of the flat and came down here. That would be about two-and-a-half years ago, as I said.'

As with the others he interviewed, Tipper raised the question of elimination fingerprints; like the others, Wallace raised no objection.

On the doorstep of the Wallaces' house, Tipper turned and nodded briefly. 'It may be necessary for us to talk to you again, Mr Wallace.' Wallace did not look very thrilled at the prospect.

In the car going back to the Yard, Markham said, 'You know, guv'nor, I think I feel sorry for that poor sod.'

'I should save your sympathy, if I were you,' said Tipper. 'There's more to that odious bastard than meets the eye. He might claim to be nearly broke, but he can run to a Porsche on the drive – and he didn't get that suit at Marks and Spencer.'

'He as good as said that his wife was financing him, guv.'

'That's what he said, but was she? She didn't look the sort to shell out for him. It wouldn't surprise me to find that he's got another source of income from somewhere, Charlie.' He paused as Markham negotiated the slip road on to the Kingston Bypass. 'Don't forget what Sheila Johnson said – that she'd done a few porn shots for Charley Godley, despite Godley's denial. That means that Penny Lambert probably did as well. It might just be that our Mr Wallace's secret was that he offered Penny a better deal, and he was making money out of her, too.'

'I'll bet his wife doesn't know.'

'I wouldn't be surprised if she did,' said Tipper. 'Even two civil servants' salaries coming in doesn't make you rich – not rich enough for a Porsche, and his sort of suits. And did you notice the Bang and Olufson stereo unit? They don't come cheap. No, Charlie, they might have been making quite a bit out of the porn business.'

'Well it wouldn't be in their interests if she got murdered, would it?'

'Meaning?'

'Meaning they'd be unlikely to kill the golden goose.'

'Depends. If they're at it, Penny won't have been the only girl they used. But she might have been trouble. What would their reaction have been if Penny had mentioned that a word to the Department of Trade about how they earned their pin-money could do them some damage – unless they upped the ante?' Tipper slumped down in his seat and stared gloomily out of the windscreen. 'They struck me as a pretty unsavoury pair.'

'It would be useful to know where they were during the weekend in question, sir,' said Markham. 'If they were away from home, then they'd need a few more answers than they've given us already.'

'That shouldn't be too difficult. I wouldn't mind having a good look round their drum, either.'

'You going to get a warrant?' asked Markham.

'Not yet, Charlie. There's not really enough evidence, but I wouldn't mind betting there's a few cameras and floodlights upstairs in that house, and a profitable little porn business going. It wouldn't surprise me to find that

Linda Wallace was featured in a few of these naughty pictures, either.'

Markham wrinkled his nose. 'I think she'd probably look better with her clothes on, guv,' he said laconically.

Chapter Seven

'If there had been a female version of Jekyll and Hyde, I reckon this Lambert woman would have qualified,' said Tipper.

'And there could be more,' said Markham. 'The most we've got so far stops two-and-a-half years ago, then jumps via the Foreign Office to a beach in Brittany. In between – nothing!'

Tipper nodded in a dispirited way. 'We've got to fill in that gap, Charlie. Not that I think it'll do any good, but you never know. For sure, if we don't bother, that's where the answer will be.'

It was then that an interesting development occurred. Fingerprint Branch identified a further mark that had been found in the flat. It belonged to the civil servant Wallace. And Wallace had claimed that he hadn't seen Penelope Lambert for two-and-a-half years. But on the evidence of Mrs Mason – and Mallory – the girl had lived in the Wimbledon flat for only nine months. Something didn't gel.

Despite the overt, macho image which Wallace was at pains to project, Tipper had gained the impression that he wasn't a man to commit murder. But that was a dangerous presumption for a policeman to make.

'Catch him when he comes out of the office – it's in Victoria Street, just across the road – and take him into the nick, Charlie. When you've got him there, give me a ring. He needs the frighteners put on him, does Mr Wallace. I'm not having some tuppenny-ha'penny civil servant trying to have me over.'

It was twenty minutes to six when Tipper got the call from Markham to say that Wallace was in the interview room at Rochester Row Police Station – and feeling very sorry for himself.

'Mr Wallace,' said Tipper, swinging a chair and sitting down opposite the civil servant. 'I am conducting a murder enquiry and I do not have time to waste listening to lies from the likes of you. So unless you want me to put you on the sheet right now for complicity in a case of murder, you'd better start telling me the truth about your association with Penelope Lambert.'

'I don't know what you mean, Chief Inspector. And furthermore, before I say anything, I want my solicitor here.' Wallace leaned against the hard back of his chair and folded his arms.

Tipper smiled patiently. 'Mr Wallace,' he said, 'you told me two days ago that the last time you had seen Mrs Lambert was two-and-a-half years ago – yes?' Wallace nodded. 'Where was that?'

'I told you.'

'Tell me again.'

'When I left the flat we shared at Battersea.'

'She was murdered about seven weeks ago. Do you know where she was living immediately before her death?'

'No idea,' said Wallace loftily.

'Wimbledon.' Tipper paused. 'And your fingerprints were found in the flat, mister.'

Wallace unfolded his arms, and his shoulders drooped. 'Oh!' he said.

'Yes – oh!'

'I couldn't very well tell you in front of my wife, could I?'

'Perhaps we'd better start again then.'

'Could I have a cigarette, please.'

'Go ahead.' Tipper didn't smoke.

Wallace took a packet of cigarettes out of his pocket and fiddled around with his lighter. He puffed smoke towards the ceiling and then looked at Tipper. 'That woman was irresistible – but so was Linda. She was working in my office at the time, and although I was living with Penny, things started to develop between Linda and me— '

'And Linda owned a house and you didn't?'

'That was purely incidental.'

Tipper was unconvinced. 'Go on.'

'Eventually I had to choose. Apart from anything else, it was costing me a fortune.' Tipper smiled. 'I moved in with Linda, and six months later we got married.'

'And what about Penny? You just abandoned her, I presume – at least for the time being?'

Wallace fixed his gaze on the tin lid that served as an ashtray. Finally he looked up. 'The trouble with Penny was that she was so damned compelling. I couldn't leave her alone. She stayed on in the Battersea flat for about six months, and I carried on seeing her.'

'This was during the time you were living with Linda down at Surbiton, was it?' Wallace nodded. 'And presumably making preparations for getting married?'

'Yes. It doesn't sound too good, does it?'

'I shouldn't think that your wife would have thought too much of it,' said Tipper drily.

'She was so vivacious.' Wallace carried on, almost talking to himself. 'I told you we'd met at a party, didn't I?' Tipper nodded. 'I started chatting her up straight away. I don't know who'd invited her – didn't care. I said I thought I recognised her, and was she an actress? That was true – I certainly thought I'd seen her before. I know it sounds hackneyed, but I really did.'

'All right,' said Tipper. 'You've convinced me.'

'She said no, she wasn't an actress, but she did adverts,

and that's where I might have seen her. Then she laughed and asked me if I knew any casting directors because she was mad to get into television. I passed that off by saying that I thought I might. I didn't tell her I was a civil servant – it's so deadly dull. Not the sort of job that would have attracted a girl like her. Anyway I dated her a couple of times – candle-lit dinner for two – that sort of thing. Got her into bed after only the second time.' He spoke as though it were some kind of creditable triumph, but noted the lack of response in Tipper's face, and went quickly on. 'Well about the fourth time we went out she said that she was looking for somewhere to live, and did I know of anywhere. I laughingly suggested that she move in with me. To my amazement, she jumped at it. Within twenty-four hours she was installed.'

'Did she know you were a civil servant then?'

'No. I told her I was something in the city – an executive. Well it was partly true, except that it was in the City of Westminster, and I was a senior executive officer.' He smiled. 'I'm a principal now, of course.' He said it as though it were important. 'Funny that, in view of what she finished up doing.'

'Which was?'

'Working at the Foreign Office.'

'How did you know that?'

'It was really me who was responsible for her getting the job. I think I told you that she stayed on in the flat after I'd left— '

'Yes,' said Tipper, interrupting, 'but you haven't said why. You had a relationship with the girl – you were living together as man and wife, and then Linda appears, and off you go. How did Penelope react to that?'

'We had a row. Not about me going. I went because of the row.'

'What was it about?'

'I was talking to a friend of mine – we play squash from time to time – and we were having a drink afterwards when

84

he mentioned this girl he'd met. He told me all about her, how they were screwing regularly and what they got up to. Then he told me her name— '

'Penelope Lambert?'

'Yes.'

'Didn't he know that you were living with her?'

'No. I didn't tell anyone, just in case it got back to the office. I was in line for promotion then, and that might have put paid to my chances. Anyway, you can imagine. I went back to the flat and had it out with her. She just laughed and admitted it. Said I wasn't married to her and what she did with her body was her business. So I told her, right, if that was her attitude, I could take the same stance, and what I did with my money was my affair, and that from now on I wasn't subsidising her.'

'What did she say to that?'

'She said I hadn't got any money – that I was up to my eyes in debts.'

'And were you?'

'Yes – still am, as a matter of fact – although why I'm telling you all this I don't know.'

'Because I asked, and because you've got some explaining to do. You were saying – you're in debt.'

'Yes. Overdrawn at the bank. Behind on the car. And all my credit cards topped up to the limit.' He laughed but didn't sound amused. 'That's life, I suppose.'

Tipper imagined the life he was talking about. He had seen the sports-car on the drive in Surbiton. He noted too the clothes that Wallace wore. He was a man who clearly attempted to create an impression with material things – a substitute for character, and a recipe for disaster.

'So you left her to it?'

'It was the excuse I wanted really. I'd met Linda who'd just got divorced – and got a good settlement. She had her own house— '

'The one you're living in now?'

85

'Yes. We got on extremely well – at first – so I proposed to her and she accepted. She suggested that I moved in straight away, and that we should get married later. Well that suited me in the circumstances, and that was that.'

'I suppose you saw that as solving your financial problems as well?'

'It certainly put an end to paying the rent – the rent on the flat. I didn't need to give Linda very much; she's working, of course. It was very much a co-operative. Linda knew I was in debt and I saw it as a chance to get straight— '

'But you didn't?'

'I didn't count on still seeing Penny. She rang me at the office one day – it must have been about a month later. Full of contrition, and how she desperately wanted to see me, and would I go to the flat and see her. Like a mug I went – couldn't resist her. Of course, the situation became worse than ever – money-wise. She was short of money – the modelling jobs weren't coming too often at that time, and I tried to help out.' He gave a caustic laugh. 'And I hadn't got any money either – still, the old credit cards are a bit elastic when they need to be.'

'That's what she was doing at that time, was it – still modelling?'

'Yes. But, as I say, terribly worried about money. We had a long talk and I told her I was in the Civil Service – I think that's the first time I ever mentioned it to her. She said that she'd considered it when she left school, but hadn't fancied it. She told me she'd done some sort of secretarial course. I suggested that she give it a try, just to tide her over. In fact, I told her how to go about it. Well, one look at her and she was in. I'll bet they didn't even ask her if she could type. She was obviously interviewed by a man.'

'I shouldn't bet on it,' said Tipper, but decided not to explain any further.

'I said that if she was careful, she could still carry on with her modelling – use a different name. She said she was using

86

her maiden name of Gaston anyway, and she was known at the FCO as Mrs Lambert, but then you know all that.'

'Despite that, you still went ahead with your marriage to Linda?'

'Yes. I know it sounds an awful thing to say, but she'd got money, and she was virtually keeping me.'

'And did you keep on seeing Penelope Lambert, immediately after your marriage, I mean?'

'No, funnily enough. It was about then that she moved out of the Battersea flat. I rang up one day and someone else answered the phone – someone I didn't know. She said that she didn't know the previous occupant at all – they'd never met – and she certainly didn't know where she'd gone to.'

'And you didn't try to find out?'

'No. I rather hoped that I'd got her out of my system. I deliberately didn't try to find her. I could have done, quite easily, mind you. I knew where she worked – well roughly – and a few judicious phone calls would have tracked her down, but— '

'But you did, nevertheless?'

'Not intentionally. I was out one lunch-time, in Victoria Street, and I met her quite by chance. I'm surprised it hadn't happened sooner, her working just round the corner so to speak. But that meeting was all I needed to set me off again, and I knew damned well that I'd have to see her again. It didn't help matters when she told me she was living at Hampton Wick.'

'Oh?'

'Well it's just over the bridge from Surbiton – too easy – and too close for comfort.'

'So you started seeing her again on a regular basis?'

'Yes.'

Tipper reflected briefly on the weakness of some men. 'And how long did this go on for?'

'Until about ten months ago. I kept ringing and there was no answer. Of course, she'd moved to Wimbledon by then.'

'What brought that about – the move to Wimbledon?'

'I don't know really. Mind you it was a pretty grotty flat she had in Hampton Wick, and it was a long way from the bright lights – that's what she used to say. I suppose she meant the modelling agencies. She was still keen to make a success of that, rather than her dreary job at the FCO. And there were the fares, too. She complained once about how much it cost her just to get to work each day. Actually, I think . . . ' He relapsed into silence.

'You think what?'

'I don't know if I'm right, but I got the impression that someone was looking after her when she moved to Wimbledon. She'd certainly become more distant – not so interested in me, almost as if she was trying to shake me off.'

'D'you mean she moved in with someone?'

'No. Rather that she'd become a kept woman. She never said as much, at least not directly. It's just that she seemed much brighter – more like the old Penny. And she stopped complaining about being short of money.'

'What was her address in Hampton Wick, Mr Wallace?'

'Twenty-seven Mexico Road – top flat.'

'What sort of modelling was she doing, as a matter of interest?'

'What sort? Just modelling.'

'I think you know what I mean. There's modelling and modelling. Now was she a straight model – advertising, or did she do the more provocative stuff?'

'I don't think so. I honestly don't know. She told me she had to be a bit careful that she wasn't recognised. She said she was always heavily made up, and usually wore a wig. And she never let them use her name in the press – they don't usually anyway.'

'You seem to have studied this at great length, Mr Wallace.'

'Not really. It was only what she told me – and don't forget I was living with her for six months.'

'How often did you visit her in her flat at Wimbledon?'

Wallace dropped his gaze. 'It wasn't on a regular basis. It was a bit more difficult than Hampton Wick. Perhaps nine or ten times while she was there.'

'And when did you last see her?'

Wallace took out his diary and thumbed through the pages. 'It was nine weeks ago.'

'You don't mean to tell me that you kept a note of it in your diary?' Tipper sounded incredulous; he never ceased to be amazed at the stupidity of some men.

John Wallace laid the diary on the table, open at the page, and with a smile on his face, pointed at the entry. 'There,' he said. 'I always wrote it as "foreign affairs meeting".' He sounded quite pleased with himself, as though he had done something particularly clever.

Tipper sniffed. 'Can't see why you bothered to write it down at all,' he said. 'Not the sort of thing you'd forget, I imagine.'

Wallace shrugged. 'I'm afraid I'm like that,' he said. 'I've always had a tidy mind.'

'Really?' said Tipper sarcastically.

'There'll be no need for my wife to know about this, will there, Chief Inspector?' For the first time he sounded concerned, and had it not been for the evidence of Wallace's fingerprints, Tipper would have been inclined to disbelieve what this rather pathetic civil servant had been telling him. He knew from experience that men who boasted of their conquests were often inventing them.

'No,' said Tipper. 'I shan't tell your wife.' But he didn't see why he shouldn't be a little more brutal with Wallace. 'Did you really have sexual intercourse with this woman?'

Wallace actually blushed. He was unused to direct language of that sort; was a master of euphemism. 'Yes, I did,' he said, as though Tipper had just called his masculinity into question. 'Why do you ask?'

'Only because I know for a fact that she was a lesbian.'

Wallace opened his mouth and closed it again. 'I don't believe you,' he said at length. 'She couldn't possibly have been.'

Tipper leaned back in his chair, his fingers drumming a little tattoo on the table top. 'I didn't say exclusively a lesbian. She was what we in the trade call bi-sexual.' And before Wallace had an opportunity to recover from that shock, he went on the attack again. 'Now, about the photographs you took. Where are they?' He had no evidence; just a feeling.

Wallace didn't answer immediately, but remained staring stoically at the table.

'I can get a search warrant if you prefer.'

'At the office – locked in my desk,' said Wallace miserably.

For a few moments, Tipper considered the implications of what he was about to do. 'I'm going to put you on trust, Mr Wallace. I want those photographs delivered to me at Scotland Yard at midday tomorrow. If you don't I shall obtain search warrants for both your home and your office. I needn't explain the embarrassment that that would cause with both your wife and your employers.'

Wallace nodded slowly. 'You'll have them – I promise. As a matter of fact I won't be sorry to get rid of them. I've been worried that someone will find them.'

Tipper had taken a chance deliberately. He wanted this man's co-operation still. Didn't want particularly to alienate him – not at this stage. Whether he really did wait until noon tomorrow for the photographs, which were probably irrelevant anyway, or whether he sent Markham to get them now, rather hinged on Wallace's answer to the next question. An answer which might put Wallace unsuspectingly, into the frame.

'How often did you go to France with Penny?' he asked.

Wallace looked up, staring at the Chief Inspector in disbelief. 'France? We never went to France. A couple of weekends in the New Forest was about all we ever managed. And that was when we were living together. We couldn't have afforded to go to France.' He helped himself to another cigarette from the open packet on the table. 'It's funny, you know,' he said, 'but she never seemed to be able to keep a man for very long.'

'Or a woman,' said Tipper acidly.

Wallace shot him a sharp glance. 'I suppose if she had a fault, it was that she was too friendly. She wasn't a one-man woman. She had to play the field.' It was exactly what Charley Godley had said about her.

'One more question. What exactly were you doing between the eighteenth and the twenty-fifth of August last?'

'Why on earth do you want to know that?'

'Because it was between those dates that Mrs Penelope Lambert, otherwise Gaston, was murdered.' The pathology report had narrowed the date much more accurately than that, but Tipper was not in the habit of giving gratuitous information to suspects.

'Good God!' said Wallace. 'You don't think I killed her, do you?'

'I don't know who killed her, Mr Wallace, that's why I'm asking the question.'

It was twenty past one the following afternoon when Markham tapped on Tipper's office door and came in holding an envelope. 'The photographs, sir. Wallace just came into Back Hall with them.'

Tipper emptied the prints onto his blotter and spread them across his desk.

'They're half plate exposures,' said Markham helpfully.

Tipper whistled. 'You can say that again. Naughty little civil servant.'

'Naughty little Penny,' added Markham.

91

'Have these been exhibited, Charlie?'

Markham grinned, avoiding the answer that so obviously presented itself. 'Yes, sir. He made a statement, and produced those as exhibits JW one to six.'

'Does he say when he took them?'

'May the tenth, sir.'

'Damn!'

'I know,' said Markham. 'Doesn't help, does it!'

They both knew that the entry in Penelope Lambert's diary that read 'J took photographs' was for the seventeenth of June.

'Is he certain of that date, Charlie?'

'Yes, sir – he had it in his diary.'

'He would have done.' Tipper reached across for a file. 'This is a copy of the statement I had taken from him last night. There's a reference in it to his visits to Penny's flat in Wimbledon. He implies, without any evidence, I may say, that she was being financed by someone else. His view was that a third party was paying the rent. But supposing for a moment, that her financial support was coming from a bit of private trading. There's a lot of it in the West End. You get these screwballs who just want to take obscene photographs of birds – that's how they get their satisfaction.'

'Mystery to me,' said Markham.

'And to me, Charlie. But she might have been making money by letting any punter who wanted to, drop by and take a few snaps.'

Markham looked dubious. 'They don't usually do that at home, guv'nor. They're like toms – they have a place in Soho.'

'They're the professionals, Charlie. This girl was an amateur – a gifted amateur certainly – but an amateur all the same. If a bloke like Wallace asked if he could take a few shots, she might just have realised that there was money in it. She was a professional model, after all. And you've only got to look at those photographs to see that she has a certain talent – even for porn.'

'So where does that get us, sir?'

'Dunno,' said Tipper with a rueful smile. 'But I'm still concerned about the other fingerprints in the flat. So far we've matched hers, Mrs Mason's – dear, uninquisitive Mrs Mason – and Wallace. There are still about three or four others we've got to identify.'

'What do we do next, then?'

'Take these.' Tipper pushed the packet of photographs across the desk. 'Take these to Photographic, get a blow-up of the best two faces – only the faces – and get one of the lads to show them round. Tell him to have a word with Clubs Office at West End Central, and the blokes on Toms; see if they can come up with someone who knew her.'

Markham shrugged. 'I think it's a vain hope, guv – you know what they're like – but I'll give it a go. You never know your luck. Bit risky though, isn't it?'

'Risky?'

'Well if she was worried about her job at the Foreign Office – and that was only when she was doing straight modelling – think what would have happened if these had got out.' He waved the photographs in the air and chuckled.

'Yeah – but don't forget that she had resigned. It might just be that she had realised that there was a hell of a lot more money in porn than diplomacy – if you take my meaning – and was going to go into it full time.'

'If that's the case,' said Markham, 'that could put an entirely different complexion on her murder.'

'How so?'

'Blackmail! Wallace is the sort of bloke whose career – and his marriage – could have been wrecked by those photographs.'

'He wasn't in them,' Tipper reminded him.

'No, he wasn't – but he had them in his possession. Now just supposing that there was someone who was in them – with her – and she put the squeeze on them. You know the sort of thing. Pay up or else.' He grinned. 'Bingo! Motive for murder.'

'Are you suggesting that it's down to Wallace then?'

'Not necessarily. He was perhaps only one of several and he hadn't any money. If she'd got her hooks into someone more important, someone whose reputation was nationally known, for instance . . . '

'Like a politician, or big-business man, you mean?'

'Yes. We've met them before, sir. Bloody good at their jobs – never get caught out, but the moment a pretty woman appears on the scene, they go all to pieces. Well it's possible.'

'Yes, Charlie – it's possible. But we're guessing. There's nothing substantial to support it. All we've got so far – apart from her sordid life-style – is a bunch of photos that Wallace admits he took. And that's all. He said that he took them, but we don't know. Perhaps he was just boasting. I must say they look fairly professional. It could have been Charley Godley who took them – she's a professional photographer. Penny might have given them to him. Or he might have nicked them when he was at her place one night.'

'But why say he photographed her if he didn't?'

'Oh ye of little knowledge, Charlie. Simple. It's no offence to take porn photographs for your own use. But theft – that is.'

'I can see why you're a chief inspector, Guv, and I'm only a sergeant.'

'Got nothing to do with it, Charlie. That's because I was industrious enough to take the exam – you were too bloody idle. Anyway, get those photographs done and put about, and get someone to start checking Wallace's statement – the one from last night. He's accounted for his movements

94

in the week leading up to Penny's death, but get someone to start talking to faces.'

'But some of his collateral is his missus – neither compellable nor competent.'

'So? I'm not thinking about calling her, and she knows about Penelope Lambert anyway, don't forget. Everyone knows how we eliminate murder suspects – there's enough crap about it on television these days.'

Chapter Eight

Twenty-seven Mexico Road, Hampton Wick, was a three-storied late Victorian house probably built at around the turn of the century. It looked unimpressive: the paintwork was an unremarkable brown; the front garden, although not overgrown, was very ordinary; and the lawn had the unmown look of so many gardens in mid-October.

The man who answered the door must have been about fifty-eight years old. He looked quizzically and uncertainly at the two detectives. 'Yes?'

'Mr Chambers?'

'That's right.' He still made no move to open the door any wider.

'We're police officers, Mr Chambers,' said Tipper and showed the man his warrant card.

'Oh!'

'May we come in?'

'Yes, of course.' He led them into a comfortable front room, beautifully decorated, and tastefully furnished – a complete contrast to the exterior.

'What a lovely room,' said Tipper.

'I'm a builder by trade,' said Chambers, clearly pleased at the compliment. 'This is my wife, incidentally.' He indicated a middle-aged grey-haired woman sitting knitting. 'These gentlemen are from the police, dear.'

'How d'you do,' said Mrs Chambers, and carried on

knitting. 'You don't mind if I carry on with this, do you?' she asked. 'It's my daughter – she's expecting in three weeks' time and I'm all behind with the baby clothes.'

'I wonder if you would look at this photograph, Mr Chambers, and tell me if you knew the girl.'

'That's Penny,' said Chambers, without any hesitation. 'Look, Mother, it's Penny.' He handed the photograph to his wife.

'Oh, yes, that's Penny.'

'Penny who?' asked Markham.

'Penny Gaston – she used to live here. Why? What's happened?'

'I'm afraid she's dead, Mrs Chambers.'

'Oh, no. Oh, how awful. Car accident was it?'

'No, I'm afraid not. She was murdered.'

Mrs Chambers put her hand to her mouth. 'How dreadful; the poor girl. What happened?'

'She was murdered in France, Mrs Chambers, and we're investigating her death. Now, can you tell me when she lived here?'

'Ah, now let me see,' said Chambers, running a hand round his mouth. 'It must have been, what – July or August two years ago.'

'It was August,' said Mrs Chambers decisively. 'It was just after Julie had her first – don't you remember?'

'Yes, of course. Can always rely on Mother to remember the date of anything,' said Chambers proudly.

'And when did she leave?'

'That would have been . . . yes, January the year after next, if you see what I mean. This January, in fact. She was here for two Christmasses. We were sorry to see her go. Such a nice girl.'

'Do you happen to know what she did for a living – at that time?'

'She was a model. She used to do those fashion poses.

97

She showed us a magazine once – a foreign one, it was. I'm not surprised, mind you – she was a beautiful girl.'

'Yes,' echoed his wife. 'A beautiful girl.' She paused for a moment, the clicking of her knitting needles temporarily silent. 'And now she's dead – what a tragedy.'

'Did she have any visitors while she was here?' asked Tipper. 'Or do you know of anyone she was particularly friendly with?'

Mrs Chambers smiled, almost conspiratorially. 'Oh, yes. Penny was in the top flat, and she got very friendly with the gentleman in the middle flat. We always call them that – top, middle, and ours is the bottom. So much more friendly than giving them numbers, don't you think?'

'Oh, absolutely,' murmured Tipper. 'Do you happen to recall his name?'

'It was Webster – Jimmy Webster,' she said.

'Is he still here, Mrs Chambers?' He glanced briefly at Markham. They had found another 'J' – perhaps the one who took photographs?

'No, bless you. He left just before Penny did. He went quite suddenly – just before Christmas. She was really upset about it.' She thought about that for a moment. 'Well not upset, but cross. No – almost a bit afraid.' She lowered her voice to almost a whisper. 'To be perfectly honest I did wonder if she was – you know, pregnant.'

'And was she?' Tipper knew that the French pathologist's report had stated the view that she had become sterile after the birth of her first and only child, but Tipper had known doctors to be wrong before – and particularly doctors who were pathologists.

'We never found out.' She looked at her husband as if expecting confirmation. 'A fortnight later and she'd gone too.'

Tipper nodded. 'You say the man Webster left suddenly. Have you any idea why?'

'His father died. He came in here one morning – this

98

very room. I remember he had a big bunch of flowers for me – he was a lovely boy. He said as how his father had died suddenly and he was going to have to go back to ... ' She hesitated and looked at her husband. 'Where was it, Dad? Canberra or Cape Town, I can't remember now.'

Tipper looked at Chambers.

'I don't know,' he said. 'I know he was foreign – well not foreign, but Commonwealth – he was white, of course,' he added, and Tipper thought that he had been about to say that he wouldn't have any blacks, but remembered that he was talking to policemen. 'I'm not good at accents,' he said. 'But I reckon he was either Australian or South African.'

'We had a row about the rent,' continued Mrs Chambers. 'He insisted on giving me a month's rent in lieu of notice, and I said that wasn't necessary. I mean, it wasn't his fault that his father had died. But he made me take it. He said it wasn't my fault either, that Dad and I shouldn't lose money just because he had to go home.' She stopped knitting, tucking needles and wool down the side of the settee. 'Then the police came about him.'

'When was that?' asked Tipper. He knew this damned enquiry was going too easily; there had to be a problem somewhere.

'A week or so after he'd gone home,' said Chambers.

'Longer than that,' said his wife in definite tones. 'It was after Christmas. Don't you remember? Penny had gone as well.'

'Where did they come from?'

'I don't know. From the local police station, I suppose. I don't remember them saying, do you, Dad?'

Chambers shook his head. 'I don't think they said.'

'What did they want?' asked Tipper.

'They didn't say,' said Chambers, reasserting himself as head of the household, and obviously the one who dealt with police enquiries. 'Just wanted to talk to him. Well he'd gone. They asked if we had a forwarding address, and

I told them what I've just told you, about his father, and going back to . . . I wish I could remember whether it was Canberra or Cape Town.'

'And they seemed satisfied with that?'

'Well they had to be, didn't they. There was nothing else I could tell them. Oh, they did ask if they could have a look round his room. We hadn't let it again. They had a quick look and went off.'

'And you heard nothing more?'

'No.'

'Would it be possible for us to have a look in the room Penny was in?' Tipper hadn't much hope of finding anything useful, but it was something which had to be done – just in case.

Chambers looked doubtful. 'Well,' he said. 'There's a new tenant in there now. A Miss Lawrence . . . '

Pauline Lawrence was a secretary in an advertising agency, she told the policemen. She wore jeans and a sweater, and no shoes. She was about twenty; of a generation which held the police in much less awe than did the Chambers downstairs. Cheerfully admitting that her flat was a shambles, she invited Tipper and Markham in and offered to make them a cup of coffee, which they politely declined.

They explained briefly that they were interested in the woman who had occupied the flat before she moved in and asked her if she had left anything behind. No, she said, the flat had been cleared out completely, but they were welcome to have a look round.

A glance round the living-room confirmed what the girl had said about its untidiness; the bedroom was even worse. Pauline just laughed and confessed that she hated housework but admitted to having a blitz about once a month. Markham reckoned that the blitz must be about due. Despite the fact that it was now gone eight o'clock in the evening, the bed was still unmade, and there were clothes spread about the room, occupying every imaginable place; on chairs, on the bed itself, on the floor, and on hangers along the front of the wardrobe. The dressing-table looked like a terrorist outrage, with bottles, make-up and aerosol tins covering every square inch of its surface.

'It's a bit untidy,' she said, with masterly understatement. She laughed again; she clearly didn't give a damn.

Tipper surveyed the room from just inside the door. It was obvious that the cataclysmic arrival of Pauline Lawrence had obscured anything which might have been of evidential value.

'There's something funny about the wardrobe,' she said.

There wasn't much of the wardrobe that Tipper could see, but he studied it nevertheless. It was a good forty years old. It had a single door in the middle, so that the cavities on either side were difficult to get at, and had a large inset oval mirror. There was a drawer at the bottom with brass handles, and at the top, an intricately carved trim. It didn't look funny to a man of Tipper's age who had seen its like in a score of seaside hotels over the years.

'What's funny about it?' he asked.

By way of reply the girl started taking clothes off the front of it and laying them on the bed. Eventually she opened the door to reveal even more clothes. 'It's the mirror,' she said. 'Look, you can see through it from the inside.'

Tipper and Markham studied it closely. From the outside, it was a normal mirror, but from the other side Tipper was able to see the rest of the room. 'Well I'll be damned,' he said to Markham. 'It's a two-way. Look, you can see where it's been fitted – and not very well.' It was evident that the original mirror had been removed and replaced by a two-way mirror, held in place by clips. On a hunch, Tipper moved the clothes to one side and peered into the wardrobe. Screwed onto the side panel was a piece of wood, and another on the other side. He turned to Pauline Lawrence.

101

'Was there a shelf in here when you moved in?' he asked.

She shook her head. 'No.'

Markham pushed his hand behind the wardrobe and after a bit of juggling withdrew a piece of unvarnished chipboard. It was about five feet long and some eighteen inches wide. 'The shelf,' he said. 'But I bet he didn't leave the video-camera behind,' he added, echoing Tipper's thoughts.

'And he won't have left any fingerprints on that, either.'

'You wouldn't get any off that texture anyway,' said Markham.

'That's what I meant,' said Tipper with a glance that implied that he knew what he was talking about. 'Nevertheless, I think we ought to get Sid and his lads down here to take a look. It's just possible that he might find one on the mirror somewhere.'

'And there again, he might not,' said Markham pessimistically.

The fingerprint team arrived within the hour and carried out a thorough examination of the flat now occupied by Pauline Lawrence. It was disappointing. The only prints were those which the police had expected to find; Mr and Mrs Chambers, Pauline, and a couple which Sid was almost certain were Penny's. The senior fingerprint officer, realising the importance of the case, had brought down the equipment for instant comparison, and had taken elimination prints from the Chambers and their tenant. For good measure they also examined the middle flat, now empty again, Webster's successor as tenant having left two weeks previously. They found some more prints identical with those thought to be Penny's and a few probably belonging to the latest tenant. They could, of course, have been Webster's, but without having a set of his they couldn't be sure.

'It's impossible to say after all this time,' said Sid, 'but it looks to me as though he made a thorough job of wiping clean. He's obviously a professional, Harry, but a professional what is anyone's guess.'

'Thanks for trying anyway,' said Tipper. Back upstairs, he turned to the girl, who had watched fascinated throughout, and apologised for the disruption.

She had made coffee for everyone, and now dismissed Tipper's apology with a smile. 'That's OK,' she said. 'It's just like the telly.'

'Not really,' said Markham. 'They always solve it in fifty minutes on the box, otherwise the advertisers get all upset. But then you'd know that in your business, I suppose.'

'And what does that all amount to, then?' asked Tipper, when they finally got back to the Yard.

'I know what it amounts to,' said Markham, 'but I'm not sure what it means. I reckon that this bloke Webster – if that's his name – put a two-way mirror in his wardrobe with a shelf across the middle. That was in the right position for a video-camera, but that's a guess— '

'Don't see what else it could have been,' said Tipper.

'But assuming it was, anyway,' continued Markham, 'What was he photographing? He's a "J" but he wasn't taking photographs on the seventeenth of June – he was already gone.'

'Gone from Mexico Road, certainly. But how do we know he didn't reappear in Wimbledon. It was a bit of a coincidence that both he and Penny left within a fortnight of each other.'

'Well we do know that she wasn't averse to the occasional exotic pose.'

'You mean porno,' said Markham brutally.

'Yes,' said Tipper wearily. 'I mean porn. I was just trying to be nice about it.'

'Left it a bit bloody late,' said Markham, half to himself.

Tipper grinned. 'What have we got then?' he asked. 'This man Webster – Australian or South African – becomes friendly with Penny, either accidentally or on purpose. Some sort of agreement is reached, and he persuades her to have a two-way mirror and video-camera installed. Now why should he do that?'

Markham shot a cynical glance at his chief. 'Come on, Guv'nor. It's got to be blackmail. What else?'

'Blackmailing who?'

'Anybody who can't afford for it to be known that he's having it off with some bird. There's plenty of punters who'd fall into that bracket.'

'But the Chambers didn't mention a stream of male visitors.'

'Frankly, guv, I think they're a bit too naive to have noticed anyway, but supposing said callers asked for Webster instead of Penny. It would suit them – and Penny. Then they keep going up the stairs, past Webster's flat to hers – at the top. And there doesn't need to have been that many – not a stream as you call it. You only need two or three carefully selected victims and you've got a nice little earner going.' Markham stretched his legs out and looked thirsty; it was nearly one in the morning and pubs were long closed.

Tipper relented, and opening the bottom drawer of his desk, took out a bottle of Scotch and two glasses. 'You can get the water,' he said.

When the drinks were poured, Markham carried on. 'There can't be any other reason for him cleaning the place out. If it was just him and her – for their own personal amusement – there's nothing illegal.'

'Then why not set up the camera on a table? Why go to all the trouble of fixing up a two-way mirror?'

'Well guv'nor, one thing's certain. We can't ask her and we can't ask Webster – until we find him.'

'If we find him,' said Tipper. 'But at least we can talk to the local nick. The Old Bill obviously took an interest in him, and he took flight almost immediately afterwards.

Something rattled our Mr Webster, Charlie, and it could have been a bit of police interest.'

'If it was blackmail, it could open up the field of our murder suspects,' said Markham, casually picking his teeth.

Tipper nodded slowly. 'I'd reached that point some time ago, Charlie,' he said.

'Neck-and-neck,' said Markham.

'Charlie, I do wish you'd stop talking in bloody riddles. What are you on about?'

'Well firstly, Wallace's statement checks out – more or less. There are one or two gaps, but not at the crucial period, and certainly not for long enough to have been to France and back.' He sucked through his teeth, and Tipper frowned. 'But Mistress Lambert – well now, that's interesting.'

'On the game?'

'Oh, no, nothing so crude. Just a few whispers that she was not averse to doing the occasional private photo call, with or without cameras, if you take my meaning, for those with the right money. At their place – West End flat, hotel room, friend's place – that sort of thing. In other words, a high-class stripper.'

'What about her place at Wimbledon?'

'Not mentioned,' said Markham. 'Perhaps that was so rare and so discreet and so expensive that no one ever got to hear.'

'Or Wallace was a one-off – for old time's sake,' said Tipper.

Markham pursed his lips. 'You do have a way with words, guv'nor. But, yes, you might be right.'

'Anything else?'

'Yes. I tracked one bloke down – exclusive high-class club; the sort of place you-know-who might go to . . . ' Markham winked. 'He said he'd heard that she would do the occasional strip, but only for a very select very private audience, and in a very private place – men or women!'

'Oh Jesus!' said Tipper. 'This bloody enquiry's getting too much for me. Why the hell couldn't we have had a clean, decent, straightforward stabbing in an East End boozer?'

'That's because they know you're good at these dodgy murders, guv'nor.'

Tipper shot a malevolent glance at his subordinate. 'What about Hampton Wick, Charlie? Any joy from the local nick?'

'Yes. The collator's off, but the station officer had a look in the index. There's a trace, but he can't understand the collator's notes.'

'Bloody terrific, isn't it. There are times when I despair of this police force. When's he back?'

'Day after tomorrow,' said Markham, picking his teeth.

'That's no good. This is a murder enquiry. I want him here today. Get him called out.'

'He's in Spain, guv.'

'Christ Almighty,' said Tipper. 'There are times when I think we pay policemen too much. When I was a PC I couldn't afford a week in Brighton.'

'I still can't,' said Markham.

'Right. We'll see your club owner first.'

Chapter Nine

The inside of Bellamys had the tawdry look of the morning after the night before. The tables were bare, shorn even of their tablecloths, and there was a staleness in the air, a legacy of poor ventilation and an excess of cigar and cigarette smoke. In the harsh daylight it was hard to believe that by evening the shabbiness would be disguised by discreet lighting, attentive waiters in evening dress, plush curtaining, and a band that was just obtrusive enough to allow intimate conversation to be unheard on the next table.

'Stewart Taylor,' said the figure behind the desk, rising as Tipper and Markham entered his office. 'I'm the proprietor.'

They shook hands and sat down, Taylor to continue stirring at a fizzing mixture in a glass.

'Rough night?' asked Tipper, nodding at the glass.

'No.' Taylor drank the mixture down with a grimace. 'I've got an upset stomach. What can I do for you, gentlemen?'

'Have a look at that, for a start,' said Tipper, laying a copy of Penelope Lambert's photograph on the desk.

Taylor withdrew a heavy-rimmed pair of glasses out of his top pocket, flicked open the arms and put them on. 'Mmmm!'

'Is that the best you can do?' asked Tipper. 'You do know her?'

'Yes, I know her, old boy. She's called Penny Gaston.' He sighed. 'But I told him that.' He nodded towards Markham.

'And when Sergeant Markham came to see you,' said Tipper, 'you also said that you had seen her in here from time to time – yes?' Taylor nodded. 'And,' went on Tipper, 'you knew her to be a strip-tease artiste?'

'Would you like a cup of coffee, gentlemen?' asked Taylor, 'because I bloody well would.'

'Yeah, fine, thanks very much.' Tipper shrugged. There was no way that this was going to be a quick interview.

A waiter brought coffee and went through the complicated routine of serving it, enquiring whether it was to be black or white, and would sir take milk or cream, and would he like white sugar or brown sugar. Eventually they got back on course, somewhat savagely.

'Can we stop pussyfooting about, Mr Taylor?'

Taylor held his arms up in an attitude of surrender. 'She used to get in here from time to time, sure.' He stirred his coffee.

'Mr Taylor,' said Tipper, his patience shortening by the minute, 'can I just say this? I am investigating a serious crime – I am not in the slightest bit interested in the law relating to the licensing of clubs, or infractions of the law, other than to say that if anyone proves to be unco-operative – even ever so slightly – I shall arrange to have him struck off and he will likely never trade again. Are we at one on that?'

Taylor spun on his chair and opened a cabinet behind him. He withdrew a bottle of Glenfiddich and three glasses. 'Got it, Chief Inspector,' he said, and poured a measure of Scotch into each of the glasses without asking. 'What do you want to know about this girl?'

'The when, the where and the how of what you told DS Markham here.'

'She came in here once or twice, well maybe a bit more often than that. To be perfectly honest I was a bit concerned about her – I thought perhaps she was a high class tom – she was in with quite a few different guys, and that sort of

108

reputation doesn't do a place like this any good, given the clientele.'

'How did you know?'

Taylor smiled – a worn, tired smile. 'The intelligence officer in a place like this is always the head waiter. If you've got a good one – and I have – he keeps you informed of everything that goes on. It's got to be. Your blokes from the Clubs Office are always poking about, waiting to pounce, and it's such a cut-throat business that any of my competitors'll put the bubble in for me without a second thought. There's no honour in this trade, believe me.'

'Where do we find this head waiter of yours?'

Taylor glanced at his watch. 'He's probably in already. He usually gets in about now. He's got an office behind the bar.' Taylor stood up. 'If you come with me, gentlemen, I'll show you, unless you want to talk to him in here.'

'No – we'll talk to him in his own domain, thanks. It'll save taking up any more of your time.' What Tipper meant was that he didn't want Taylor there when he talked to the head waiter.

The head waiter's office was little more than a cupboard, and the middle-aged grey-haired man who stood up when they entered was introduced by Taylor as Pierre. He inclined his head slightly and murmured 'M'sieur' to each as the introductions were made.

'Thank you, Mr Taylor,' said Tipper by way of dismissal, and the owner left, somewhat apprehensive about what his head waiter might say in his absence. Taylor was not a happy man.

Pierre brought in a chair from the main room of the club, and all three sat down. It was crowded. 'What can I do for you, m'sieur?' The head waiter spoke with a French accent.

'Peter Morton, isn't it?' asked Tipper brutally. Markham had done his homework in his enquiries at the Clubs Office.

The head waiter knew when he was beaten. He paused, sighed, and said, 'What can I do for you, guv?' in tones that bore greater proximity to Hoxton than to the Seine.

'How often did you see this girl in here?' Tipper laid the photograph on the desk in front of Morton.

'Five or six at most, I suppose.'

'Who was she with?'

'Other people's husbands probably.'

'Names?'

Morton looked wounded. 'This is a discreet place, guv'nor,' he said. 'That's the way the punters like it.'

'I'm not too interested in what the punters like,' said Tipper. 'I'm investigating a murder – her murder, and I'm getting a little impatient with being buggered about at every turn.'

'Christ!' said Morton. 'I didn't know that she'd been topped. When did that happen then?'

'Never mind. Who were these blokes?'

'I honestly don't know. The waiter on the table does the bills up, but I reckon it's too late to find out now. It might be possible, though.' He looked doubtful, and Tipper wondered if he was playing for time.

'A lot of the trade in here is on credit cards – the old plastic money, but you can always tell when they want to be anonymous – they pay cash. That way there's no record. They're usually the blokes who worry about their reputation – those who've got a reputation to worry about, that is.' He smiled sarcastically. 'There was only one of those, at least he was the only one I remember – the only one I dealt with. We were a bit pushed that night – one of the waiters was off sick, and it was a Saturday, so I had to do a bit on the tables myself.'

'Hard luck,' said Markham, in an aside.

'And who was he?' asked Tipper.

Morton shook his head. 'Well I don't know, do I? I mean, that's what I was saying, isn't it? He wanted to remain anonymous.'

'Seen him since? Has he been in again?'

'Yes.'

'With a woman not his wife, I suppose.'

Morton looked reproachful. 'The most charitable view you could take is that it was his daughter – and if she was I can understand him not wanting to let her out of his sight.' He smirked.

'When he was in here with Penny Gaston, did it look like an evening out?'

'He didn't pick her up in here, that's for sure. And they left early – by our standards anyway – like they were going on somewhere else.'

'Did you put them in touch in the first place?'

Morton looked searchingly at Tipper. 'Look, guv'nor, I've got a living to make here. If I blow the whistle on the punters they're going to go some other place, and then I'll be out on my neck, and what's more it'll get known on the circuit, and I'd never get another job.'

'That might just happen anyway,' said Tipper threateningly.

Morton's anxiety manifested itself in a gentle wringing of the hands. 'I'll do what I can to find out,' he said reluctantly.

'Good,' said Tipper. 'I'll wait.'

'Jacob – Richard Jacob.'

Tipper nodded. 'Just jot down the address for me, will you?' He pushed a note-pad across the desk. Morton only hesitated briefly before getting out his pen.

'This don't have to go no further, does it, guv?'

Tipper stood up and shook his head. 'No,' he said, and placing the palms of his hands flat on Morton's desk leaned towards him. 'And if Mr Jacob discovers that we're interested in him before we tell him, there can only have been one bloke who told him.'

Morton placed his right hand on his chest approximately where he believed his heart to be. 'Stand on me, guv.'

'I might just do that,' said Tipper menacingly.

*   *   *

It was no surprise to Tipper that Jacob was an importer and exporter, a term which, to his sceptical mind, covered a variety of nefarious activities.

Tipper reflected, as they were shown into Jacob's elegant office, that the enquiry into Penelope Lambert's untimely death was getting just a little monotonous. The murder of a Foreign Office secretary, and its investigation, was revealing at every turn, a secret life that left, at the end of each interview, further questions unanswered. There were times when he felt that for every step forward he was taking two back.

And each interview seemed to start in exactly the same way. 'Can you tell me when you last saw this girl, Mr Jacob?' The same photograph was slid across the desk.

Jacob picked it up and stared at it, his bottom lip slowly protruding as he thought about what he ought to say in order to leave himself as uninvolved as possible. He laid it down again, but continued to gaze at it. 'How far does this information have to go, Chief Inspector?'

'Mr Jacob,' said Tipper, 'I am not in the business of trading. I do not haggle for information. I have a variety of weapons in my armoury, like arrest warrants, search warrants, witness summonses – each of which has to be obtained in open court, and inevitably attract the attention of reporters who have little else to do but hang around the courts of this country waiting for the snippet that will keep them in good with their editors, to say nothing of the gossip columnist who might just buy them a drink.' It wasn't strictly true, of course; it was ages since Tipper had obtained a warrant of any sort in open court. He tended to see the magistrate in his private room, or even at home. But there was nothing to stop him. What he didn't explain to Jacob was that to do so would, in most cases, be counter-productive to the enquiry. But it was good enough.

112

'About three months ago.' Jacob spoke in resigned tones, his shoulders visibly slumping. He looked very miserable.

'Would you care to elaborate on that?'

Jacob glanced at Markham, sitting to one side and busily making notes, and sighed. 'I've got a flat in town that I keep for entertaining . . . '

Tipper raised an eyebrow. 'Have you?'

'It's not what you think,' said Jacob.

'You don't know what I'm thinking.'

The heavily-ringed fingers of Jacob's podgy hands intertwined on his blotter. 'I often have businessmen over from abroad, but discussing things is not always easy in a restaurant. I've got this flat – penthouse, it is – and I get one of these executive caterers, girls that have done the cordon bleu bit, and they come in and provide a meal for us, and afterwards we can get down to business. Talking prices and agreements – that sort of business,' he added hurriedly.

'And where does she fit in to all this?' Tipper extended a finger towards the photograph which still lay on Jacob's desk.

Jacob turned his hands over so that they lay now palms uppermost on the blotter. 'Chief Inspector, you're a man of the world.'

'So people keep telling me,' said Tipper. 'And they say it in the hope that I'll overlook some breach of the law.'

'Some foreign businessmen expect more. It often makes the difference between clinching a deal and not. You see they're used to that sort of thing abroad.'

'What sort of thing?' Tipper knew; he just wanted to hear it from Jacob.

'A stripper.'

'And that's where this girl came in, is it?'

Jacob nodded. 'She was quality stuff, not the sort of slag you can pick up anywhere round the village – you

113

know, Soho. You've got to be a bit careful. You don't want someone who's going to come back at you and try and put the arm on you – you can do without that sort of aggravation.'

'And how did you find her? She wasn't a professional.'

'That was partly the attraction. I had a quiet word with Pierre, the *maître-d* at Bellamys, to see whether he could do anything. He told me about this bird.' He nodded at the photograph. 'He fixed it all up. I went along to the club one evening, bought her a few drinks, fixed the price, and bingo. She didn't come cheap, mind you, and gave me all the usual crap about not doing it as a living, and being selective – all that.'

'So you engaged her?'

'Yes – unfortunately.'

'Oh! Not value for money?'

Jacob looked balefully at Tipper, trying to detect some trace of amusement behind the Chief Inspector's bland expression. 'A bloody disaster as it turned out. She practically wrecked the whole deal.' He shook his head wearily as though the memory still troubled him. 'She was good that girl, very good. And tasteful. I don't think I've ever seen anything quite so provocative; genteel and teasing.'

'What went wrong then?'

'One of my bloody guests did. She'd taken everything off and was gyrating round the room, just a fraction out of reach – you know the way they do, but one of the idiots reached out and touched her. In fact he tried to grab her. I'm not surprised, mind you, after her performance.'

'And?'

'She went absolutely crazy. There was nothing in it, of course – these continentals are used to being able to do that, but she obviously didn't think so. She was like a wildcat, shouting and screaming at him. Then she grabbed

114

him between the legs and squeezed – hard. Then it was his turn to scream . . . '

'I should imagine so,' murmured Tipper.

'She was shouting by now, something about "And how do you like it when someone does it to you?" Well he was on the settee clutching himself and moaning, and she was about to go for him again, when I grabbed hold of her from behind and lifted her bodily away from this bloke. She cooled down a bit then, and I went round collecting up her clothes and apologising. Then I pushed her into the bedroom and told her to get dressed and get out.'

'You paid her?'

He spread his hands in a gesture of helplessness. 'Of course I paid her. She's the sort of cow who'd have sued me in open court.'

'I doubt it,' said Tipper.

'Ah, but you can never be sure – it's not worth the risk. Actually, I gave her a bit more because she was going on about it not being in the contract – getting touched, I mean. I thought it might keep her quiet. Anyway, why are you asking all these questions?'

'Because someone decided to keep her quiet permanently, Mr Jacob. Someone killed her.'

For a moment, Jacob sat stock-still at his desk, hands palm-down, his spatulate fingers spread. 'That such a thing should happen! It must have been a man. She hated them.'

'Why do you say that she hated men?'

'You could tell. Her performance that night. I said it was good, and it was, but it was contemptuous – sneering almost.'

'Aren't most strippers like that?' asked Tipper. 'I don't think they've a great deal of time for mere males.'

'I know all about that,' said Jacob, 'but this girl, well there was definitely something more. A hatred.'

'Like a lesbian hates men?'

Jacob nodded slowly. 'Yes,' he said. 'Exactly like that.'

'Were there any Frenchmen at this select little party of yours, Mr Jacob?'

'Frenchmen? Why on earth should you ask . . . ?'

'Because she was murdered in France.'

'You don't think— '

'I'm not thinking anything – I'm enquiring. Now, any Frenchmen?'

He shook his head. 'No, no Frenchmen.'

'Would anyone who was there have been likely to see this girl again, afterwards? Could they have been at Bellamys some time after and recognised her?'

Jacob smirked. 'I doubt it – they weren't looking at her face.' Neither Tipper nor Markham smiled, and Jacob looked immediately serious again. 'Frankly, if they had seen her again I should think they would have run a mile – in four minutes. Anyway they all went back the next morning.'

'All? How many?'

'Three.'

'And where did they go?' Tipper began to feel as though he was extracting teeth – without gas.

'Düsseldorf.'

'And were they all Germans?'

'Yes.'

'Names?'

Jacob knew the question was coming, but hoped that it wouldn't. He held up his hands. 'Mr Tipper,' he said pleadingly. 'I've got a business – a reputation. What are you asking? Why do you want these names?'

'Because I'm going to have them interviewed by the German police – that's why.'

'Please, Mr Tipper . . . '

Tipper looked round the opulent office. 'Of course, we could get a search warrant, if you prefer, and interview all your clients until we get down to the right ones. Might take time, but we've got plenty of that.'

'All right, all right.' Jacob stood up and walked across to the door. 'Dora, get me the file on that order we did with Graz of Bonn.'

Jacob found the three names in the file and jotted them down on a piece of plain paper. 'Please, Mr Tipper, be discreet, eh?'

'Don't worry, Mr Jacob. The German police are the soul of discretion.' He handed the piece of paper to Markham. 'Afterwards – after she had wrecked your little party – what happened then?'

'She went home.'

'She didn't stay for a drink?' Tipper asked with a smile on his face.

'You must be joking. As soon as she was dressed, I put her in a cab.'

'Where was home? Where did she go?'

'I don't know. I didn't ask and she didn't say. It's better that way.'

'You must have heard what she said to the cabbie.'

'She didn't say anything. She got into the cab and went. She probably did it deliberately so I wouldn't hear. Told the driver the address once they were on the move.'

It didn't matter too much; Tipper knew where she was living then. 'When did you see her again?'

'Never. I didn't see her again. Never wanted to.'

Tipper paused and then spoke as though struck by an original thought. 'Did you take any photographs of her?'

'Photographs – me? What would I want with photographs of her? No thank you – I just wanted to forget her. That woman was bad news, Mr Tipper, believe me.'

Tipper sighed. That was another 'J' who could have taken photographs but denied it; curiously he believed this one.

'I don't think I've ever been involved with an enquiry that came to so many dead ends,' said Tipper.

117

The enquiries that the German police had made on behalf of the British police who were making enquiries on behalf of the French police had come to nothing. It was exactly as Jacob had said – well almost. The three German business-men had been interviewed and had confirmed the account of Penny's strip-tease performance. The only difference was that the man whom Jacob had said grabbed the girl denied having done so. He also denied that she had grabbed him and severely bruised his testicles in the process. But that didn't surprise Tipper, and didn't really make any difference to the enquiry overall. The German police, with typical Teutonic thoroughness, had verified the whereabouts of the three men for the weekend of Penelope's death, and were able to say that all three had been in Germany. Finally they sent a set of fingerprints for each of the men they had interviewed.

'That was good of them,' said Markham.

'Yes,' said Tipper, and smiled as he thought of a macabre exhibit in the Black Museum downstairs. Some time ago Scotland Yard had asked the German police for a set of fingerprints from a dead body. They had sent the arms.

None of it added anything to the hunt for the Lambert girl's killer. And Jacob's fingerprints – Tipper didn't bother to get a set from him; had known that they were already on record at Scotland Yard before they interviewed him – did not match any of those found in Penny's flat. It was as if they were back at the beginning again. Which in a sense they were.

'I'm bloody sure that blackmail's got to be at the back of this somewhere, Charlie.' He let out an exasperated sigh. 'Here we've got a girl employed at the Foreign Office of all places, who's moonlighting as a stripper, a photographic model, and probably a bit of selective tomming as well. She's bi-sexual, has got her hooks into a civil servant in the Department of Trade, and is secretary to some big-wig, what's his name: Mallory, and finished up getting herself topped in Brittany. It stinks!'

'It's a familiar pattern, sir,' said Markham. 'A few naughty pictures of her and her fancy man of the moment in bed together, and then the screws go on.'

'Exactly. But how the hell do we get at it. Mallory and Wallace would both be terrified of the publicity if it got out – and both would probably lose their jobs, and their wives probably; though in Wallace's case, I shouldn't think he'd be too sorry.' Tipper reached for the phone and dialled the number of the fingerprint officer dealing with the Lambert case. 'Sid, remember telling me that the half-print you found on the camera recovered from the ferry matched one of the sets on the letter of resignation? Have we got any further with that?'

He put the phone down. 'Dammit!' he said simply.

'No joy?' asked Markham.

'No!' Tipper sat in contemplation for some minutes. 'The answer's got to be there – in the Foreign Office somewhere, Charlie. If that print on the camera matches one of the sets on the letter, then someone from the FCO might just have put the luggage on the ferry. And that someone's got some answering to do.'

'And it's not Penelope Lambert's print?'

'No it's not – Sid's quite adamant that her prints do not appear on the letter.'

'I don't understand that,' said Markham. 'How the hell can you write a letter of resignation and not get your prints on it. Unless she wore gloves.'

'Why should she do that?'

'Unless she was trying to set someone up?'

'Don't see it, Charlie. Christ, man, no one sits down at a typewriter with gloves on – and you don't sign a letter with gloves on.'

'So what do you deduce from that, sir?'

'That she didn't write the letter, Charlie.'

'Where do we go from here, then?'

'We pursue our enquiries, as they say. First of all, get alongside that bird who's now doing Penelope's job, what's her name, Deidre, or something?'

'Not bad, guv. It's Kate McLaren.'

'Yeah,' said Tipper, 'I knew it was something like that. Get hold of her – not literally, of course, and find out the procedure for resigning. What happens. Who the letter's normally written to, who it's given to, and what departments it has to go through. That sort of thing. And anything else that might come in useful. Chat her up. That sort of thing. Got it?'

'Got it,' said Markham, not too displeased at having to take a girl out to dinner on expenses.

'It seems,' said Markham, 'that a letter of resignation goes to the Establishments Department at the Foreign Office. It can go through the bloke you work for, or you can just tell him you're doing it. The Establishments people pass it around – pensions – that sort of thing, just to check if she's entitled to anything like a repayment of the contributions they don't make in the first place,' he said sarcastically. In common with all policemen, Markham resented having to contribute eleven per cent of his salary to buy a pension that everyone else got free.

'In other words, we're no further forward.' Tipper thought for a moment or two. 'If her fingerprints aren't on the letter, it probably wasn't written by her.'

'She could have got a typist to do it for her,' said Markham.

'Christ, Charlie, she was a bloody typist – of course she would have done it herself.'

'Supposing she didn't. Just supposing she got another girl to knock it out for her and just signed it. She could have done that without getting her dabs on it.'

'Give me a bit of paper – out of that cabinet there.' Tipper pointed to a small cabinet of drawers containing all the stationery that detectives might need to get through a working day. 'Now, put it in front of me, as though you were a typist bringing it in for signature, and see if I can sign it without getting my prints on it.'

Markham slid the sheet of A4 onto Tipper's blotter and he signed it two-thirds of the way down, about where Penelope Lambert's signature appeared on her letter.

'There you are,' said Markham. 'All you'll have got on there is the side of your hand, and there's no trace of that.' He held the side of his palm in front of Tipper's face. 'See, guv. It's smooth beyond the palmprint – which we haven't got anyway.'

'There's a lot of assumption gone into that, Charlie. I still can't see that she would have let someone else type it, still less would she have let someone else hold it. Look. If I take it normally, there'd be prints on the edge where I took hold of it, and then there'd be almost a full set somewhere on the left-hand side where I'd held it firm while I signed.' He demonstrated by putting a second signature on the sheet of paper.

Markham shrugged. 'Yes, I suppose so. So we'd better make some enquiries – find out if there's anyone there who did type it.'

Tipper shook his head slowly. 'Not if it's a forgery. I don't want to put them on notice that we're interested. Anyway who would have wanted to forge it – who could have forged it?'

There was a brief silence, then both detectives spoke at once. 'Mallory!' they said.

For a moment they both sat considering what they had just said, and wondering why they hadn't said it before.

'But he said he hadn't seen the letter,' said Markham.

Tipper sucked through his teeth. 'I have known people to tell lies before, you know, Charlie,' he said sagely.

'This is true, guv. What do we do now, go and have a chat with him?'

Tipper smiled. 'Not bloody likely. You've met him. He's as cunning as a . . . ' He paused. 'As cunning as a diplomat.'

'But if it was him, and let's face it, sir, we're a million miles away at the moment, but if it was him – why?'

Tipper shrugged. 'The oldest reason in the book, I should think. The other woman. Darwin, Godley and Wallace all said she put herself about a bit. Jacob says she was a stripper. Chummy – what's his name in the night club?'

'Taylor.'

'Yeah, Taylor. He said it as well. A stripper for men and women.' He pondered on that for a moment. 'I can just imagine an audience of lesbians leching over her.' He stopped again. 'Come to think of it, though, I can't really. But then again, Charley Godley, the dyke photographer, reckons they had it off together for six months. Makes you wonder where, and if, Mr – soon to be Sir Robert – bloody Mallory fits into it all.'

'I think you've just said it, sir.'

'Said what?'

'Soon to be Sir Robert. Try this for a scenario,' said Markham. Tipper winced; he hated buzz-words, and 'scenario' was one of his aversions. 'Supposing Mallory was having it off with Penelope. Nice body – nice flat – nice set-up. Perhaps she puts pressure on for a bit of stability – marriage. Mallory can see his bloody precious knighthood blown out of the water by that sort of scandal – after all there is a bit of form for it in and around Whitehall. So goodbye Penny Lambert, née Gaston.'

'Who's "J"?' asked Tipper.

'What – "J took photographs", you mean?'

'Yeah. It's got to mean something. We're pretty sure that her lovely body got photographed fairly regularly, so what's so special that it merits an entry in her diary. That

122

bugs me, Charlie. Every time we get somewhere – or think we do – I always come back to this "J" finger.'

'And we've still got three sets of marks in the flat to identify.'

'And one of them is on the letter and on the camera.' Tipper blew a raspberry. 'Once we've identified that lot I reckon we've cracked it, Charlie.'

'But how, sir? We can't just steam in and ask for Mallory's dabs.'

'No, we can't, Charlie. There's got to be another way.'

Chapter Ten

The other way turned into one hell of an argument between the Commanders of Scotland Yard's C1 Branch and its C11 Branch.

Tipper belonged to C1, which among other things, undertook the sort of international murder enquiry in which he and Markham were becoming more and more involved. C11 was the branch that gathered criminal intelligence, ideally before the crime, rather than after it, and they had arguably the best surveillance team in London, although Special Branch would have disputed that. Special Branch, however, tended to keep a low profile, and preferred not to offer themselves up for the sort of assignment that the Commander of C1 Branch was now busily trying to sell.

The Commander of C11 was a dour Scot – the Commander of C1 an educated cockney. C11 was called McGregor; C1 was called Finch.

'It's no good appealing to my better nature,' said McGregor, 'I don't have one.'

'But it won't be for long,' said Finch. 'For Christ's sake, Mac, I'm not asking for the bloody earth.'

'You are in my book, Colin. But I'll see what I can do.' He looked unwaveringly at Finch. 'Isn't this a risky business you're getting into here, Colin? Putting surveillance on a senior official at the Foreign Office.'

'I don't give a damn what he does for a living. He's a murder suspect— '

'It's a bit thin.'

'Of course it's thin. How many murders have you investigated in your career where the evidence has been thin, but they've gone down eventually?'

McGregor nodded and then smiled. 'Aye, a few, I suppose.'

'Well then!'

'But for the most part they've been domestics, or a brawl outside a boozer somewhere – nobody like this bloke. Supposing he susses out he's being followed?'

Finch scoffed. 'Are you saying that your blokes are so unprofessional that he'll spot them?'

'No, of course not.'

'Well, there you are, then. This bloke Mallory's not a pro. It'll never even cross his mind that we've put a team on him.'

McGregor scratched the side of his nose thoughtfully with the stem of his pipe. 'A week then. But if anything else crops up, it's finished – I'll have to take them off – switch them.'

'Make it a fortnight, Mac.'

'Look, I've said— '

'Case of Scotch?'

'Ach, the hell with you, Colin Finch. All right, but if anything else— '

'You're a lovely man, Mac.'

'Piss off!'

Detective Inspector Henry Findlater was also a Scot, which caused Sassenach detectives to accuse Commander McGregor of running a Scottish mafia. It was always an unwise observation; it allowed him to make odious comparisons with the English. Findlater was fresh-faced, short, barely meeting the minimum height requirement for the force, and wore,

125

on occasion, horn-rimmed spectacles, which gave him the appearance of being a student. But he was astute, and particularly nimble on his feet, both of which were attributes for the successful surveillance officer. The team of sixteen which he led were sergeants and constables whom he had trained himself. Many had sought to join his élite squad, but there had been a fair number of disappointed applicants. The appeal of belonging was a strange one. The hours were long and arduous; the work boring and tedious; but their successes over the years had been legion.

Findlater stood now in front of them, briefing them about their latest assignment. There were five women and eleven men, remarkable only for their unremarkable appearance. It was a common mistake to assume that surveillance officers would disguise themselves as punks or that the women on the team should be pretty. In reality they shunned any characteristic that would draw attention to themselves; they must not allow a quarry to realise that he had seen a particular officer perhaps ten minutes previously, or yesterday – or last week. There were common factors though. Each member of the team was intelligent and quick-witted, physically fit – and dowdy.

The official car carrying Robert Mallory turned out of King Charles Street and left into Whitehall. Mallory sat in the back, wearing glasses and reading some papers which he exchanged from time to time for others in the despatch box which lay open on the seat beside him.

Following his car through the rush-hour traffic was an easy task for the motor-cyclists on the team, but they abandoned it once it reached the more open and less crowded roads of Buckinghamshire, leaving the observation to a trio of very ordinary cars which leap-frogged each other to assume the prime position during the journey. When it became apparent that Mallory was making for home they left him to be 'booked in' by a casual pedestrian who happened to be passing the entrance to his driveway as his car swept in.

The next morning the surveillance team took Mallory to work again, but Findlater's problem, which he explained to Tipper later, when he gave him what was to become a daily briefing, was that he didn't know what he was supposed to be looking for. It was, as Tipper explained, a speculative operation.

'In a sense, Henry, it's a fishing expedition.'

Findlater smiled. 'Yes, I'd worked that out for myself, guv'nor, but what are we hoping to achieve? This man is a murder suspect, right?' Tipper nodded. 'It's not my place to ask how or why you came to that conclusion – it's your business, but it would help if you could put down some markers. What d'you want?'

'I don't know, Henry. To be perfectly honest, I suppose I'm hoping for some abnormality of behaviour, some indication that our Mr Mallory is not the perfect diplomat – just something.'

Findlater took off his glasses and rubbed at them with his handkerchief, a mildly puzzled expression on his face. He put his glasses back on and peered at Tipper as if seeing him for the first time. 'Not much help, sir, if you don't mind my saying so. It might be more productive if we leaned on him a bit.'

'Leaned on him?'

'Sure – let him know he was under observation. See if it panicked him a bit – yes?'

'No!' said Tipper. 'He's not that sort of man. I've interviewed him once. He's supremely confident; he doesn't rattle easily. The only effect of letting him see we were taking an interest would be a complaint of harassment – and probably straight to the Commissioner. I don't mind that, but it would mean taking the obo off, and I don't want to do that yet. The least I'm hoping for

127

is some indication of his life-style. To see if there are any cracks.'

Findlater shrugged. 'Well, it's your job, sir. My team'll do their best. See you tomorrow.'

Findlater's team started to establish the pattern of Mallory's normal daily routine. With some difficulty they unobtrusively covered all the entrances to the Foreign Office. At lunch-time, Mallory emerged and strolled casually along King Charles Street and descended the Clive Steps. He crossed the road and did a circuit of St James's Park, regularly nodding to acquaintances, of whom there appeared to be an inordinate number but, as Findlater said when he received the report, it was not surprising. When one had worked in the Whitehall area as long as Mallory, one got to know a surprising number of people, if only distantly. What had to be avoided, Findlater told his team, was being misled by them, and taking off on the pointless pursuit of some casual contact. Surveillance was a disciplined business.

In the case of Mallory, it was not only disciplined, but was used as a vehicle for gathering information about him, and the background enquiries which could be made as a result of learning a little more about him each day.

On the fourth day there was a variation in the pattern. The target left the office earlier than usual, but went straight home. Findlater kept a nondescript vehicle near the Mallory house and was rewarded at about seven o'clock when the official car reappeared. Mallory emerged from the house in a dinner-jacket and ushered an attractive woman into the car. Findlater knew already that this was Lady Francesca Mallory, a daughter of the late Earl of Homersham, and sister of the present earl. That much one of his beavers had learned from a few hours at the General Register Office at St Catherine's House. Mallory and his wife drove to the Egyptian Embassy where local enquiries of the Diplomatic Protection Group indicated that the ambassador was hosting a select dinner-party. Mallory and Lady Francesca went home again at about eleven and Findlater's officers went home too.

The following day the normal pattern was resumed. To the office, a walk round the park, and home again. The only thing to occur that was different was the arrival at the house at the same time of a Porsche sports-car which pulled into the drive behind Robert Mallory's car. A young man, whose age the watchers put at about twenty-eight, got out and exchanged a few words with Mallory before both went into the house. A check of the car's index mark against the police computer showed that the keeper of the car was a Sean Pearce whose address was shown as Princes Risborough.

The log of the surveillance team showed that Pearce came out of the house again about twenty minutes later accompanied by a young blonde girl who, although a little on the plump side, was nonetheless quite attractive. This they assumed, rightly, to be the Mallorys' daughter, Tessa.

On a hunch – what he called the just-in-case syndrome – Findlater decided to leave the Mallorys' house under observation the following day while Robert Mallory was at work. It paid off, even if it didn't prove that Robert Mallory had anything to do with the death of Penny Lambert. That afternoon, when Robert Mallory was known to be ensconced in his office, Sean Pearce reappeared, this time on foot. He was admitted by Lady Francesca and left again about two hours later, leaving a comfortable gap of about an hour before Mallory got home from work. He walked some way before driving off in the Porsche which he had parked judiciously some way away.

At his dourest, Findlater merely nodded when he read that part of the report.

Tipper was a little more forthcoming. 'What a crafty ladyship,' he said. 'If Lady F's having it off, then it wouldn't be surprising to find that her old man's doing the same.'

Findlater looked dubious. 'That doesn't follow, sir,' he said. 'Anyway, we don't know for sure that they were having it off.'

Tipper smiled. 'I'll put money on their not having spent the time playing Trivial Pursuit.'

'Depends what you mean by trivial,' said Findlater drily, and Tipper blew him a kiss.

On the following Monday, Lady Francesca drove to Victoria and parked her Rover in one of the back streets of Pimlico. She then made her way confidently to a small flat and let herself in with her own key. She spent about two hours there before returning to Chalfont St Giles. More background enquiries were made and the flat was found to be a pied-à-terre rented by Sean Pearce. Tipper contemplated the enigma of her not going to Princes Risborough because it was too close to home, but happily going to Pimlico, less than half a mile from where her husband was working.

That too was resolved by enquiry. At Princes Risborough, Pearce shared a house with his widowed mother.

All of that was very interesting, and supported Findlater's Calvinistic view of what he described as the upper classes, but it contributed little to the case against Mallory.

'Fascinating, isn't it?' said Tipper. 'Young Sean turns up and takes Tessa out to night clubs and discos, and then in his spare time, to coin a phrase, he pops back and gives her ladyship a seeing-to. Must be on Benzedrine.'

'Bloody disgraceful,' said Findlater mildly. 'These are the people who're running the damned country. It's downright immoral.'

Tipper smiled. 'Let he who is without sin, et cetera . . . '

130

'Anyway, guv'nor, I reckon that's about it. We've kept this obo going for a fortnight now, and you must admit that nothing's come out of it. Nothing that's any good to you.' He paused and rubbed his nose. 'If I'd been in the matrimonial enquiry business, I'd've made a fortune this week and no mistake.'

'Early days, Henry – early days.'

'That's as maybe, but it's a fortnight, sir, and our time's up.'

'Not quite,' said Tipper. 'My guv'nor's talking to your guv'nor – see if we can't keep it going for another week.'

'Bloody hell, sir. What're you trying to do, bore my blokes to death?'

'Patience, my son,' said Tipper. 'Complicated murder enquiries are not solved in a couple of weeks.'

'But what are you hoping to get out of this?'

'I don't honestly know, Henry. Call it instinct, if you like, but there's something about this bloke Mallory that just gives me a feeling in the bones. I'm sure he knows more than he's prepared to say. It's the letter – the letter of resignation – that worries me. How can a girl submit a letter of resignation without her own fingerprints on it, and then go to France on holiday – and not come back? No, Henry, I want to keep it on.'

'If my reading of the Police and Criminal Evidence Act is right, Charlie, we can get a warrant from a circuit judge to examine Penelope Lambert's bank account.'

'Are you sure, guv? I thought— '

'If you're going to say that we've got to have substantial evidence of her having committed an offence, you're wrong. Part Two, Section Nine, allows us to do it. And it's got nothing to do with whether she's committed a serious offence – so long as someone has.' He pointed to his bookshelf. 'There's Stone's – look it up for yourself.'

'You're right, sir,' said Charlie, when eventually he found what he was looking for. 'But you're going to have to get the warrant – I'm only a sergeant - it's got to be at least an inspector.'

'I knew there'd be a bloody catch in it somewhere. Never mind – all these things are sent to try us.'

They had already discovered from examining her papers in the flat that Penelope Lambert had two bank accounts – one in that name at a local bank, and another in the name of Penny Gaston in a bank in the West End. They saw Judge Harper in his room at the Central Criminal Court, and, after some hard and factual talking, convinced him that a warrant was pertinent to their enquiry.

The Penelope Lambert account was very ordinary. It showed the transactions they expected. Payment of salary every month, and the usual outgoings that settled household bills – rent, telephone, electricity, car insurance, BUPA, and housekeeping. It was the Penny Gaston account they found interesting. It stood at a few pounds under four thousand, a sum that had accrued over the last two or three years, and was made up of irregular payments of about two to three hundred pounds a time.

'I don't understand why she left all that in a current account,' said Tipper.

'I do,' said the manager. 'If she'd transferred it to a deposit account or a building society, she'd have had to pay income tax on the interest.'

'So what?'

'I don't know what you're looking for,' said the manager, 'but from what you say, she may have thought that her employers would have found out in some way – perhaps through a substantial change in her tax coding.' He spread his hands. 'They wouldn't, of course. The Inland Revenue couldn't care less so long as you pay what you owe them. They're not the slightest bit concerned that you're breaching

132

your conditions of employment by moonlighting.'

Tipper laughed. 'I've heard it called some things . . . ' He stood up. 'Thanks for your help,' he said. 'I think we've got what we need – although God knows what it means, other than she had what appears to be a profitable sideline going. It's amazing what the female body can earn if it's used in the right way.'

'Or the wrong way,' added Markham with a smirk.

'It's beginning to come together, Charlie,' said Tipper.

The Metropolitan Police has an unerring ability to select inappropriate titles for the various tasks its officers undertake. One such title was that of collator – just that, collator, which means one who collates. Simple. But the Metropolitan Police does not define what he collates – at least not in the title. A better description would be divisional intelligence officer, but that conjures up a picture of a red-tabbed colonel sitting in a military headquarters somewhere. So perhaps collator will do.

The collator at the police station which included Mexico Road within its boundaries was a man of about fifty. He had served the Commissioner for some twenty-nine years and quietly boasted that very little occurred on his division that he didn't know about. And he had a comprehensive card index system to prove it.

'I believe you were making enquiries about a Jimmy Webster of Mexico Road, sir,' said the collator, when Tipper and Markham entered his office.

'What d'you know about him?' asked Tipper.

The collator produced a card from one of his many drawers and laid it on the desk in front of him. 'Oh yes, I remember this one now. Got pulled by the area car just before Christmas – immediately before Christmas really. It was on the twentieth – a Friday – at two o'clock in the

133

morning. It was a suspect drink-drive by the look of it. Ah, that's a bit of luck.'

'What is?'

'Saunders and Ritchie – the terrible twins were on that night, and they're on now. D'you want to have a word, sir?'

'Yes, please – if they're get-attable.'

'No problem, sir.' The collator turned to his personal radio and called the area car crew.

Within about seven minutes Saunders and Ritchie – driver and wireless operator respectively – had joined Tipper, Markham and the collator in the latter's tiny office. In common with all policemen suddenly summoned to see a strange chief inspector from the Yard who was accompanied by a sergeant, they assumed that they were the subjects of some disciplinary action, or at best a complaint; chief inspector was the rank that normally investigated such matters. They were, therefore, somewhat relieved to hear, not only that Tipper was investigating a murder, but that, to the best of his knowledge, no complaint or disciplinary action had emanated from it.

'Jimmy Webster, middle flat, Twenty-seven Mexico Road. You stopped him on the twentieth day of December at two a.m. , according to the collator.' The driver, Saunders, nodded. 'What was it all about?'

'I remember that one quite clearly – Hampton Court Road from Hampton Court towards Kingston Bridge. Got his foot down – really hammering. That's a dodgy bit of road that – had a few fatals in its time. Got to have been on the bevvy, so we gave him a pull. Looked like a straight breathalyser job, sir.'

'And was it?'

'No it wasn't.' He paused. 'D'you mind if I smoke, guv?'

'Go ahead.' Tipper waved a hand.

134

'Like I said, we gave him a pull. Usual questions, like have you been drinking, sir – all that. He said no, then he said well perhaps one. Anyway, to cut a long story short, we gave him the test . . . '

'Yes?'

'Negative. I reckon he was lucky, or the wind was blowing in the wrong direction. I was about to let him go with a verbal warning for speed, when Don here weighed in.' The driver turned to his colleague.

'Well I'd been listening to him talking, this guy,' said Ritchie. 'And I was fascinated by his accent. Then it clicked. I said to him "You're South African, aren't you?", and he said he was. Didn't seem too happy about it though, sir. But I've got this sort of ear for accents. So we had a little chat. I asked him how long he was over here for – was he a resident, working here, that sort of thing.'

'And?'

'He didn't want to give me a straight answer to anything. We did a check on the car, but that was all right. It came out on the computer as down to him, and the address was right. But there was something I wasn't happy about, sir. D'you know the feeling I mean?'

'I do indeed,' said Tipper, who called it policeman's nose. 'But what did he actually say – can you remember?'

Both the policemen hesitated, thinking. 'It was getting on for ten months ago – longer even,' said Ritchie. 'But I asked him where he was going. That was easy. He was going home. Then I asked him where he'd been. Near Windsor is what he said, and when I asked him where exactly, he hedged a bit, and said something about meeting a mate in the middle of the town, near the castle, and following him in his car to a pub. Usual thing, sir. He didn't know the name of this pub, and wasn't sure exactly where it was, and no, he didn't think he could take us there. Then I asked him where he was working, and he said he wasn't – not at the moment. That seemed a bit odd, because he was driving a BMW – well you don't push those around when you're on the dole, do you, sir?'

'Some of us don't even drive them when we're working.' said Tipper with feeling.

'Anyway we decided to have a look in his motor.' He glanced at Saunders, as if seeking confirmation for his actions. 'That's when we found the video tapes.'

Tipper's eyes narrowed. 'What video tapes?'

'There were four of them in the boot of the car. The minute we turned those up he started to get quite animated. He started asking us about our powers of search, and then said they were private and wouldn't be of any interest to us. Funny that, the way people react: if he'd said they were four episodes of Coronation Street, or something like that, we'd probably have slung them back in the boot and told him to go on his way. But there was something – I don't know what, but you just get that feeling, like I said before.'

'So what did you do?'

Ritchie looked sideways at Saunders – the older of the two. The driver smiled. 'We nicked him, guv.'

Tipper smiled too. 'What for?'

'Well we didn't actually nick him, not in the true sense. We just told him we weren't satisfied, and that we were taking him down to the station for further enquiries to be made.'

'What did he say to that?'

'Nothing much. I suppose he thought he could talk his way out of it – whatever it was. He was probably thinking that that would give him time to work out some excuse that would satisfy us. But he was certainly a bit nervous about those tapes.'

'So you took him to the nick – in here, in fact?'

136

'Yes, sir. And by the time we'd got here he'd recovered a bit. The usual thing – saying we couldn't hold him; he'd done nothing wrong, and he wanted his solicitor. All the usual old madam in fact. Anyway, we dumped him in the interview room, told the station officer what we'd got – or at least, what we thought we'd got, and then we nipped upstairs and borrowed the Chief Superintendent's video.' Saunders laughed. 'Well, I suppose you can guess, sir? Porn!'

'What sort of porn?' asked Tipper.

'It was nothing professional. It was a tape of some bloke having it off with some bird – quite juicy it was.'

'D'you think that this film was taken from one position?' Saunders laughed. 'One position?'

Tipper laughed too. 'You know bloody well what I mean. Was the camera in one place all the time?'

'Yes – sorry sir. Yes, it was. And it was a bit misty – sort of filmy, if you'll excuse the pun. Bit like it had been taken through a piece of dirty glass.'

'A two-way mirror maybe?'

'Yes, indeed. That's exactly what it was like.'

'Was the bloke in the film Webster?'

'No, sir. Don't know who it was but he was quite a performer. And the bird – she was something else – great.'

'Who was this girl? Any idea? Or the man?'

'No – 'fraid not. We put it to him, of course, but he wouldn't say a word. He said it was no offence to have them – that it was no offence to take them, and that was all he was going to tell us. Then he said he wanted his solicitor, and that we should either charge him with something or release him.'

'Did you just look at the one tape?'

'Yes, sir. We guessed that the others were all the same, but I suppose we should have had a dekko.'

'So what happened then?'

'We had a word with the night-duty CID, and he said there was nothing we could put him on the sheet for, and the best idea was to have a word with Special Branch on account of he was South African, and might be an illegal immigrant, and he might even be in the porn trade, even though the tapes we'd got seemed to be private ones, if you know what I mean. Anyway the station officer bailed him – police bail pending further enquiries, and told him to report back here in twenty-eight days.'

'And did he?'

'I don't know, quite honestly, guv. We handed the tapes over to Special Branch and let them get on with it. I don't know whether anything came of it . . . ' He paused. 'Just a minute, though . . . ' He turned to his colleague. 'Didn't he skip, Don?'

'Yes, I remember something about that,' said Ritchie. 'The SB bloke – a skipper, I think he was, came and saw us. Yes, that's right. He'd apparently been back to this bloke's drum, and he'd scarpered – back to South Africa, he said. He was thrashing about trying to get some more details. He asked us if we'd seen a passport, or anything like that. Well, we couldn't help him – we hadn't even seen a driving licence; I remember that because we issued him with a form to produce that, his insurance, and test certificate . . . ' He glanced at Saunders. 'Or did we? No, no test certificate. It was practically a new car. That's about it, guv.'

'You don't remember the name of this bloke in Special Branch, by any chance?'

'No, sir.'

'No matter,' said Tipper. 'We should be able to track him down easily enough. Incidentally, did he say whether this bloke was of any interest to them?'

Ritchie grinned. 'No, guv. They never tell you anything, those blokes.'

'Where are the video tapes now?' asked Tipper.

'We handed them to Special Branch. As far as we know, they've still got them, sir.'

'Did she look as though she was a professional at this sort of game?'

'I don't know about professional, sir, but she certainly looked as though she was enjoying herself.'

'Doing it for a living maybe?'

Saunders nodded slowly. 'You could be right,' he said. 'I reckon that those four tapes-worth would have been worth a bob or two to her.'

Chapter Eleven

But Tipper's ponderings on Penelope Lambert's alternative source of income suddenly took second place to what
emerged next.

The Commander of C1 Branch had managed to secure
a third week's surveillance, but only by a great deal of
cajolery and bribery, the more commendable because he
too was beginning to agree with the Commander of C11
Branch that the watchers were wasting their time.

On the last day but one of that third week, the surveillance team, now in danger of becoming lethargic because
a pattern had been established, were shaken out of their
professional reverie.

Mallory emerged from the Foreign Office at half past
twelve as usual, and walked through the archway into King
Charles Street. But instead of going down the Clive Steps
and into the park, he turned left, across Whitehall and into
Westminster tube station.

'Blimey, someone's shaken the kaleidoscope,' said one
of the watchers enigmatically.

The surveillance officers were not close enough to hear
Mallory ask for a ticket. It wasn't crucial, because they
travelled anywhere on the London Underground on their
warrant cards; but it would have been helpful to know in
advance where he was going.

Mallory caught the first eastbound train that came in,

and oblivious to the police officers surrounding him, rode to the Embankment. He made his way quickly through the station – so quickly in fact, that for a moment the team thought that he had spotted them – and onto the Northern Line platform. There he waited while trains for High Barnet and Mill Hill East came and went.

'Looks like it's the Edgware train he's after,' said one of the team into the microphone secreted in his sleeve.

Minutes later his assumption was confirmed. Mallory sat down on one of the long seats, spending his time assiduously reading the advertisement cards, unaware that the disinterested yob standing not six feet from him was a detective sergeant from the Criminal Intelligence Branch.

Ten minutes later, Mallory alighted at Mornington Crescent. He stopped briefly outside the station, and spoke to a news vendor who, seconds later, was shaken to discover a warrant card thrust under his nose. 'What did he want, guv?'

'Blimey, mate, watch me 'eart. He arst fer a boozer in Malplaquet Street. Why? What's 'e done?'

'He's a hopeless alcoholic,' said the detective, moving on swiftly, and broadcasting Mallory's destination through his personal radio so that some of the team could be there ahead of him.

Two of the surveillance team were already at the bar drinking pints by the time Mallory walked in. He was clearly apprehensive; the clientele in this particular pub was not the type with whom he normally mixed. He bought a gin and tonic and sat down at a vacant table in the corner not far from the door.

The remainder of the team stayed in the street on the orders of Henry Findlater. 'I'm not having all you buggers getting pissed on the firm's time,' he said. He knew policemen very well, which was as it should be.

For the next five minutes or so, Mallory sat, occasionally sipping his drink and wishing that he had bought a newspaper. Then a woman walked in. She was about five feet nine inches tall and wore white slacks and a navy sweater that did nothing to disguise her shape. She walked confidently up to the bar and ordered a drink. She turned and ran a hand through her short brown curly hair. Then without hesitation she crossed to Mallory's table and sat down. He half rose, but relaxed again at a gesture from the woman.

One of the two police officers in the bar drained his glass and clapped his colleague on the arm. 'Cheers, mate,' he said. 'See you again.' He ambled out of the pub and told the DI what had happened. It was certain that after so discreet a meeting, Mallory and the mystery woman would split up before leaving, and the surveillance team would wish to follow her to find out who she was.

After some twenty minutes of intimate conversation during which the woman appeared to do almost all of the talking, she stood up, nodded briefly, and walked out, leaving Mallory white-faced at the table. Whatever she had said to him had shaken him badly.

Most of the team were now deployed to follow the woman whose white trousers and height were a gift for the followers. A couple of the team were left to take Mallory back to the office, which is where they were sure he would go, but followed him just the same – in case.

The woman walked quickly to Mornington Crescent station and boarded a southbound train. She alighted at Embankment and went out of the Villiers Street exit and across into Northumberland Avenue. As quickly as before she strode towards Trafalgar Square, skipped through the traffic, across the Strand and into the large building on the corner.

One detective, chancing his arm, followed her into the building. The woman held a pass out to the security guard and walked straight through, but the same guard stopped the detective. 'Can I help you?' he asked.

'Is this Canada House?' asked the policeman, knowing full well that it was not.

The security guard smiled bleakly at the stupidity of the general public. 'No,' he said, 'that's on the other side of the Square. This is the South African Embassy.'

Harry Tipper always got the impression that he was entering a rarefied area of Kew Gardens whenever he went into his Commander's office. According to the stark architectural specification, it was three modules – about twelve feet by fourteen – but softened by wall-to-wall carpeting. To these basic essentials of police command, Finch had added a vast number of potted plants which decorated the radiator grilles, the small table, the top of the bookcase; and on his desk, set at an angle across the corner of his room, stood a Devil's Ivy which spilled over the edge. The slats of the venetian blinds were aslant to permit the light but obscure the view; and a green-shaded desk lamp cast a pool of light on to the leather-edged blotter. Colin Finch liked a bit of couth in his office.

'Come in, Harry,' said the Commander, in response to Tipper's gentle tap on the open door. He looked up expectantly.

'Bit of a problem arisen on this French job, sir – the Lambert murder.'

'This going to take long?' The Commander put down his pen and linked his fingers together. 'Shut the door.'

'I'll make it as brief as I can, sir.' And Tipper outlined the enquiry to the point where Mallory's meeting came to the notice of the surveillance team.

Finch smiled. 'I'm pleased about that,' he said. 'Mr McGregor was starting to take the piss a bit about that job.'

'The next thing is to identify the woman, sir.'

'And I suppose you want to borrow the C11 surveillance team to do it?'

'Well sir, it would be— '

143

'Forget it, Harry.' Finch leaned back, his arms hanging limply down the sides of his chair. 'Don't you realise what you've got here? You've got a senior Foreign Office bloke who makes a meet with a bird in some grotty boozer in Mornington Crescent, and afterwards he goes back to his office – and she goes to the South African Embassy. What's that – some sort of bloody coincidence? What's she doing going in there, with an office pass? He's married, you say?' Tipper nodded. 'Well that wasn't a clandestine meet to have it off, was it? Because they didn't. That would have been a hotel job – quick bang-bang, and back to the office. But what did they do – have a chat, you said – yes? No, Harry, I think your lot have stumbled on to something that might just be a bit interesting. Could be a bit deep. Know what I mean? And there's enough there to be interesting. After all, the South African Embassy's in Trafalgar Square, and the Foreign Office is less than half a mile away – and she – and he – both went to Mornington Crescent, and then travelled back to more or less the same place, but not together. No, Harry, my son, that's all a bit dodgy.'

'Well what do we do next, sir?'

'You wait while I make a phone call.' Finch opened the top drawer of his desk and ran his finger down a list of numbers. Then he tapped out four digits on his telephone.

'Frank? Colin Finch. One of my DCIs, Harry Tipper, has just come in with a tale that might interest you. Have you got a minute if I send him up?' Finch listened for a while and then, obviously talking about something else, said, 'No, I didn't go. Good do was it?' He replaced the handset. 'Go up to the eighteenth floor' – he pointed to the ceiling – 'and see Mr Hussey – Commander Special Branch, and tell him the tale.' By way of dismissal, he picked up his pen. 'Let me know how you get on,' he said as Tipper opened the door.

Frank Hussey was big, grey-haired, and wore heavy horn-rimmed spectacles. He stood up as Tipper entered his office

144

and extended a hand. 'Come in and sit down, Mr Tipper. Mr Finch tells me you've got an interesting story to tell me.'

'I don't know, sir, but he seems to think that it might be of interest to your Branch.' For the next few minutes, Tipper recounted details of the enquiry, starting with the finding of Penelope Lambert's body in Brittany by Colonel Matthieu, the identification, the tortuous unravelling of her past, and finally the meeting between Mallory and the unknown girl who had gone from Mornington Crescent to the South African Embassy.

Commander Hussey had said nothing throughout, his chair sideways on to his desk, his legs crossed, and the fingers of his right hand playing an occasional and silent tattoo on his blotter – the only item on an otherwise clear desk top.

'That it?' Hussey swung round, square-on to the desk.

'Not quite, sir. There's another South African connection which has only just come to light. One in which one of your DSs was involved, I believe.'

'Oh? What was that about?'

Tipper outlined what he had learned from the two constables, finishing with the apparent rapid departure of Webster for South Africa.

'Well, well,' said Hussey. He turned to the telephone and tapped out four numbers. Waiting for an answer, he said, 'I think we can resolve that now.'

The Detective Chief Superintendent who entered the office was called John Gaffney. He was in his mid-forties and had been in charge of the Special Branch international squad since his promotion some two years previously.

'Busy, John?'

'Always, sir.'

'Well you're going to be a bit more busy now, I suspect. I want you to listen to what DCI Tipper here, from C1, has to say.' He turned to Tipper: 'I'm sorry – Harry – isn't it? Could you run through the story again, for Mr Gaffney's benefit.'

Gaffney listened intently, occasionally nodding as though what he was hearing had a familiar ring about it. When Tipper had finished, he said, 'The skipper in question was DS Ron Marshall – I'll get you to talk to him in a minute.' He turned to Hussey. 'I think we'll have to ask Harry to hold off – at least until we've had a word with the Security Service, sir.'

Tipper looked dismayed. 'This is a murder enquiry, sir,' he said to the Commander.

Hussey held up a hand. 'I know that,' he said. 'We're not asking you to stop altogether; just to wait. There may be a plausible explanation for Mallory's behaviour, but I have grave reservations about that. And if there is something sinister, as I suspect there may be, our enquiry may overtake yours: in fact, may help you to clear up your job. D'you follow?'

Tipper nodded. 'Yes, sir, of course. But may I at least follow up this business of the videos?'

It was Gaffney who spoke. 'We can do that now. From what you've been saying, it may well be connected. Once you start opening up something like this, there's no telling where it might lead.'

'We often get the Uniform coming up with things like this, sir,' said DS Marshall. 'The moment they find a foreigner's involved in anything, they think we ought to take an interest.' He smiled tolerantly. 'Our own fault really, I suppose. We never tell anyone what we're up to. Half the time we don't know ourselves.' He put his hand on the pile of video tapes on the table. 'We were on the point of destroying these. They've been skulling around in the property store for ages.'

'Perhaps for a start we could have a look at them,' said Tipper.

'Of course,' said the Sergeant. 'You won't find much of

interest on them, though, sir. Professionally speaking, of course – unless you're from the Vice Squad.'

Tipper shook his head. 'Straightforward murder,' he said. 'Well murder, anyway. On second thoughts, I'm not so sure about the straightforward bit.'

The Sergeant put a tape into the video-player and switched it on. The opening scene was the bed in Pauline Lawrence's flat, and was obviously taken from the wardrobe, from exactly the place that Tipper had surmised the camera would be on the shelf. Two naked bodies came into view. Only their backs could be seen to begin with, but then they got on to the bed and started writhing, introducing to the sex act some quite original contortions. For a good two or three minutes the woman's face was obscured by the man's body, until at last she moved and Tipper let out a sigh.

'That's her,' he said. 'That's Penelope Lambert alias Gaston. Well, well, well!'

'Seen enough, sir?' asked Marshall.

'Not yet,' said Tipper. 'If this is what I think, it would have been of no value to her unless her partner's identified.'

A few moments later the man rolled off the girl's body and unwittingly faced the camera.

'Christ!' said Markham. 'It's only bloody Mallory.'

'Are they all the same – these tapes?' asked Tipper.

Marshall turned from the video-player with a laugh. 'Yes, sir. Together they run to about two hours or so – and all as boring.'

'I meant are the same two people in each video?' asked Tipper snappily. He was beginning to tire of this supercilious dandy.

'Oh I see. No. Same girl – different partner, as I recall. Long time since I looked at them.'

'I have a feeling,' said Markham, 'that we're about to meet some old friends.'

The other three tapes were put on. Tipper told the

147

Sergeant to fast-forward each to the point where the man's face was revealed. They were not surprised to see that one of them was John Wallace, the civil servant, and only mildly surprised that Richard Jacob was another.

It was the fourth tape that stunned them, and they saw it all through for the very simple reason that Penny Gaston's partner on this occasion was a woman – but not a woman they knew.

'Oh Christ!' said Tipper, running a hand through his hair. 'Now what?' He turned to the Special Branch Sergeant. 'What was the outcome?'

Marshall opened the venetian blinds. 'Nothing! We went to his address a couple of days later to make some more enquiries but he'd gone – vamooshed. The couple in the house . . . ' He paused for a moment.

'Chambers?'

'That's them, sir, yes. They said he'd had to go back to South Africa urgently – some story about his father dying. We did a few checks, more out of interest – but nothing. Immigration had nothing – no trace of his having left the country, at least not in the name of Webster. We traced a driving licence in that name and address, but that proved nothing. No trace all round. We even checked with the Security Service to see if he could have been South African Security.'

'And?'

'If he was, they hadn't heard of him – at least not in that name. It keeps coming back to that – identification. But that could have been the reason for his disappearance. Suddenly coming to the notice of police, even though it was through something silly like this.' He gestured towards the pile of tapes.

'The girl performing on the tapes was a secretary at the Foreign Office. Lived in the flat above Webster. And she's our murder victim,' said Tipper mildly. 'Furthermore, the man on the first tape is her boss – soon to be appointed an ambassador it's said, and the bloke on the second tape is a senior civil servant at the Department of Trade.'

The Sergeant paled, his overbearing self-confidence shattered. 'Christ!' he said. 'We didn't know that.'

'And it seems to me, young man,' said Tipper brutally, 'that you did nothing to find out. And yet you say you thought Webster might have worked for South African Security.'

'I shouldn't ever apply to become a real detective.' Markham couldn't help hurling a gratuitous insult at Special Branch whenever the opportunity presented itself.

'It could well be that she was murdered by any one of the men on those tapes – or Webster.' Tipper hammered his point home. 'To say nothing of the anonymous lesbian,' he added.

'Good God!' Marshall was suddenly very apprehensive; someone might suggest that he hadn't dealt with the Webster enquiry as thoroughly as he should have done. This DCI from C1 sitting opposite him with a sardonic expression on his face was probably one of the many CID officers who thought that Special Branch was a collection of tossers. 'I think I'd better let Mr Gaffney know about that,' he said.

Tipper smiled. 'Good, because I shall be telling your Commander,' he said with a certain amount of satisfaction.

The Sergeant looked unhappy.

John Gaffney, meanwhile, had set up an incident room and made a number of telephone calls. He had devoted some time to the selection of a suitable sergeant for the office; major incident enquiries, like many other aspects of police work, were only as successful as the administrative support they received. An efficient sergeant, controlling a well organised office, was the officer who supervised such enquiries; get a poor organiser and you never recovered from the inevitable chaos of the first twenty-four hours.

149

The result of the telephone calls was the convening of a conference at that stark grey building in central London that is the headquarters of the Security Service. Present were the Director of the branch that handles counter-espionage, two members of his staff, MI5's legal adviser, and Detective Chief Superintendent John Gaffney with his Commander, Frank Hussey. In the corner was the self-effacing Andrews, leader of the watchers – the MI5 surveillance team.

'We have absolutely nothing on this,' said Carfax, the Director, with a sackcloth-and-ashes expression on his face that implied that he should have known. 'And the first priority, clearly, is to identify the woman. As you say, Frank . . . ' He nodded towards Hussey. 'It may be a coincidence that she went from Mornington Crescent to the South African Embassy. To be perfectly honest, that would have been a very silly thing to do if there is any information being passed by Mallory to the South Africans and she is the contact - very silly indeed. But then, as we know, people do do some very silly things.' He smiled blandly at the others.

Hussey was tempted to mention Bettaney, the MI5 officer who had put a note through the letter-box of a KGB man at the Russian Embassy in London offering his services, but thought that this was probably neither the time nor the place. 'Do you want any help from us?' he asked.

'I think that we can take the identification on at this stage, Frank,' said Carfax. 'Or more precisely, John Andrews can.' He looked across at the watchers' team-leader. 'Yes, John?'

'We've started,' said Andrews. He was a practical, down-to-earth fellow, and disliked Carfax's posturing.

'Ah yes, of course. Good.' For a moment or two he stared down at his notes. 'In the meantime, we have launched a thorough enquiry at the Foreign Office, to see what, if anything, our friend Mallory knows that could be of value to the South Africans.' He turned to one of his assistants, a pale desk officer called Monk. 'Is there anything yet, Charles?'

'The Foreign Office is a maze,' he said, a distasteful expression on his face, as though it were an organisation with which he would rather have no dealings at all. 'But it seems that he is in charge of one of those difficult departments that has a variety of responsibilities.' He shook his head. 'All very untidy. One of the tasks he has is something to do with the economics of South Africa.' He leaned forward earnestly. 'But just what relevance that has is a bit of a mystery – at least at this stage.' He stopped, the inflection in his voice making it sound as though there were more to follow, but nothing came.

For a moment or two Carfax waited expectantly, and then said, 'Ah yes, thank you, Charles.' He glanced across at Delaney, the legal adviser. 'Anything you want to say, Dudley?'

'You haven't said anything yet that leads me to believe that this chap Mallory has committed an offence,' said Delaney with withering lawyer's logic. 'So the answer is no.' Hussey smiled to himself.

'Mmm, quite so,' said Carfax, unwilling to take on the lawyer. 'Well for the time being, gentlemen, that seems to be about as far as we can go. Shall we meet again, say the day after tomorrow?'

'What for?' asked Hussey, cross at having had his time wasted at a totally unnecessary conference. 'Personally, I am not at all impressed by the fact that the South Africans and the Foreign Office are involved. I know they're both highly emotive to government, but as far as I am concerned, at worst it's a breach of the Official Secrets Acts, and John Gaffney here is quite capable of dealing with an OSA job.' He scowled at the assembled Security Service representatives. 'Come to think of it, I'm not too sure that I shouldn't perhaps have put a detective superintendent in charge of it.

And I might just do that if it turns out to be nothing. So many of these scares do.'

'Bloody waste of time,' said Hussey, as he got into his car. 'Where are you going, John, Waterloo?'

'Yes, sir.'

'Hop in,' said the Commander. 'I'll drop you off. It's the least I can do for wasting your time as well.'

It took the Security Service watchers three days to identify the woman. And that, they subsequently discovered, was because she'd had two days off from the office. But on the third day she left South Africa House, walked to a nearby car park, and led them quite unsuspectingly to her house in Hendon. It was a matter of simplicity thereafter to check the diplomatic index and discover that her name was Eva van Heem, a single woman of thirty-three, and a second secretary at the embassy.

'So what do we do now?' asked Gaffney of the assistant director upon whom Carfax had put the responsibility of the day-to-day running of the enquiry in conjunction with Special Branch.

'We wait and see, I suppose.' Hector Toogood stood up. 'We could go and have a beer.'

'That's the best suggestion that your lot have made so far,' said Gaffney. 'Why don't we do that.'

Chapter Twelve

The Head of the Foreign Office walked through the archway from the quadrangle just as the anonymous black car containing the Director-General of the Security Service drew into the kerb outside Number Ten.

'Good morning, John.'

'Good morning, Edward.'

The policeman had already rung the door bell, and together the two men entered the front hall. The messenger took Sir John Laker's light fawn overcoat and umbrella and hung them on the stand by the famous leather watchman's chair, and then preceded them down the long corridor that led to the Cabinet Room and the private office.

The Prime Minister's principal private secretary, Ronnie Mansell, hurried towards them. 'Sorry, sorry,' he said. 'We're upstairs this morning.' Mansell, a fussy little man, always spoke in the plural whenever he mentioned the Prime Minister.

He led the two men up the staircase, past the gallery of former prime ministers, not strictly in the order they had held office, because some had upset the system by coming back after a break, like Baldwin, MacDonald, Churchill and Wilson. And at the top, facing visitors with a look of reproachful smugness, Spencer Perceval, one of the only two prime ministers to have been assassinated.

The other, as John Gaffney knew only too well, was Radford Fairley.

Across the landing they processed, to the west side of the old house. The principal private secretary tapped lightly and opened the door of the study.

'Sir John Laker and Sir Edward Griffin, Prime Minister.'

'Come in, come in. Good morning.' The Prime Minister shook hands with each of them. 'Do sit down.'

The two officials sat, side by side on the settee, feeling a little like Tweedledum and Tweedledee. This was not going to be an easy interview. The Prime Minister moved a high carver chair and sat facing them, thus achieving a physical ascendancy. It was a typical politician's ploy.

'Well, and who's going to kick off?' The Prime Minister smiled – dangerously. 'Sir Edward?'

The Director-General of the Security Service took a metaphorical deep breath. 'We believe there may be a leak at the Foreign Office, Prime Minister.'

'Oh dear!' A slight frown settled on the Prime Minister's brow. Mansell, seated further away, looked on with a bland expression on his face, hoping there would be no blame which could be attributed to him.

'It's rather a complex story, Prime Minister— '

'Well perhaps you'd better start at the beginning.'

That had been Griffin's intention, but he was trying to devise a way of minimising the French involvement, something he knew would displease the PM.

'Towards the end of August the body of a young woman was found in Brittany which, at first sight, appeared to have been a straightforward drowning accident. However, the autopsy revealed that that was not the case. The woman was almost certainly murdered. After some time, she was identified as a Mrs Penelope Lambert, a personal secretary at the Foreign Office – secretary, in fact, to Robert Mallory . . . '

154

'Do I know him?'

'It is possible that you may have met, I suppose,' said Griffin.

Mansell coughed deferentially. 'Unless I'm very much mistaken, Prime Minister, Mallory's in the New Year List for a K.'

Sir John Laker nodded miserably. 'That is so,' he said. It was just like Mansell to rub salt in the wound. The New Year's Honours List need not have been mentioned at all. That was something that could have been dealt with quite adequately between officials – afterwards.

'The British police were asked to help,' continued Griffin, 'and uncovered some rather unsavoury details about Mrs Lambert's background and er – sexual proclivities— '

'She was positively vetted, I suppose?' asked the Prime Minister.

'Well, yes, but— '

'But not very satisfactorily, it would seem.' The Prime Minister glanced at Laker.

'I don't think, regrettable though it is, that that is germane to the matter in hand,' said Laker.

The Prime Minister tutted softly. 'Really.' The word came out flat, neither statement nor question. Laker felt uncomfortable.

Griffin struggled on. 'To cut a long story short, an observation was mounted, based merely on some video-recorded evidence that Mallory was having an affair with his secretary – who, as I have said, was Mrs Lambert. It's quite amazing— '

'Doesn't that sort of thing usually happen in the Foreign Office then?' asked the Prime Minister tartly. 'It seems to happen just about everywhere else.'

Laker sighed inwardly. He had been right to assume that this was not going to be easy. 'During the course of this observation, Mallory was seen to go to a rather inferior public house in the back streets of Mornington

155

Crescent where he was joined by a woman. Nothing took place between them— '

'I should hope not – not in a pub,' said the Prime Minister, mischievously.

'I meant that nothing was seen to pass between them – like documents or photographs. It was just a quiet talk, so it seemed, lasting about twenty minutes. The woman was later identified as Eva van Heem – a second secretary at the South African Embassy.'

The Prime Minister looked from Griffin to Laker and back again, as if expecting either one of them to continue. 'Well, is that all?'

'So far, Prime Minister.'

'Oh, I see. Well what exactly are you saying?'

'It seems suspicious— '

'Suspicious of what? He could be having an affair with this woman, as well as with his secretary could he not – or do you definitely rule out multiple affairs at the F and CO, Sir John?'

Laker smiled thinly. 'Of course it's possible, Prime Minister, but why go to Mornington Crescent to have a drink?'

'Where do you suggest – the Athenaeum?'

'No, Prime Minister, but she is South African.'

'This Mallory – is he married?'

'Oh, yes, Prime Minister, he's quite normal— '

'I was not enquiring whether he was homosexual,' said the Prime Minister sharply. 'I should hope that that sort of thing could be detected by positive vetting these days – if nothing else.' This time it was Sir Edward Griffin who, quite unjustly, was the recipient of a censorious glance. 'I was merely suggesting that if Mallory was married, and was having an affair with this woman, albeit a South African diplomat, then clearly he would wish that affair to remain clandestine, particularly as he is in the running for a K. And he must know that, as you seem to run a roster for honours at the Foreign Office, Sir John.'

Laker remained silent; the Prime Minister could be very perverse on occasions.

'So what happens next?' The Prime Minister raised an eyebrow.

'We are mounting a full-scale enquiry, naturally.'

'Naturally. With the assistance of Special Branch – the full assistance, I trust.' The Prime Minister had great faith in Special Branch.

'Of course, Prime Minister.' Laker hadn't much alternative. He would have preferred not to have to wash the Foreign Office linen in public – albeit a restricted public, but as it was the Metropolitan Police who had alerted them to a possible scandal, he had no option.

'I wish to be kept fully informed.' The Prime Minister stood up; the interview was over. 'And I think it might be a wise precaution if Mallory's name was removed from the New Year's Honours List, Ronnie, at least until this matter is resolved, don't you?'

'But isn't that rather condemning him in advance?' asked Laker.

'An honour is an honour, Sir John, not a reward for promiscuity, whatever you may think at the Foreign Office. There have been enough errors in the past.' The Prime Minister smiled – a fleeting and ingenuous smile. 'Anthony Blunt, for instance.'

It was raining when they left.

Chapter Thirteen

John Gaffney put a home-made 'Engaged' sign on his door and closed it. 'If I don't do that, I have everyone imaginable traipsing in and out of here. Sit down, Hector.'

Hector Toogood lowered himself into an armchair and, pulling a bunch of keys on a chain from his pocket, unlocked his heavy leather government-issue brief-case. 'Not good news, I'm afraid,' he said, riffling through the pile of papers.

Gaffney waited implacably, a half-smile on his face.

'It would appear,' continued Toogood, when he had found the piece of paper for which he had been searching, 'that our Mr Mallory heads a section of the F and CO that monitors the economics of South Africa, and in particular, the effect that sanctions are likely to have if imposed by us, and that are already imposed by the USA.'

Still Gaffney made no comment.

'And in order to do so, he has advance knowledge of what is likely to be withheld next by the Americans, and what we're thinking of.' Toogood looked up, quizzically.

'Oh, dear,' said Gaffney, turning his swivel chair slowly from side to side. 'I'm only a simple policeman, but I suspect that that sort of information might be of inestimable value to the Pretorian Guard.'

Toogood did not find the pun amusing, and confined himself to nodding seriously. 'Indeed it would.'

'If they're getting it,' said Gaffney. 'Is there any evidence that they are?'

'No. Not so far.'

'Can we be certain?'

'No we can't. That's the next part of the operation.' He consulted his papers again. 'We've put an intercept on his telephone— '

'Office and home?'

'Er – home. No point in putting one on his office phone. He wouldn't dare pass anything from there . . . '

'Don't be so bloody naive, Hector. He quite likely would – just on the assumption that you lot would think that he wouldn't.'

'But surely— '

'But surely nuts! Think about it. Anyway, what are we doing – playing at this or not?'

'I'm not sure that the DG— '

'Oh, balls! Hector, for Christ's sake. Either we're going to do this job properly or I'm not going to play.'

'All right. We'll put it on his office phone, too.' He scribbled a few notes on his papers, and looked up again. 'Now – surveillance . . . '

'Yes?'

'We've got two teams. One is dogging his every footstep, and the other is waiting in case he gets a call in the middle of the day— '

'On his office phone!'

'All right, John, you've made your point.'

'What about planting – have you planted anything yet?'

Toogood looked pensive. 'That's more difficult. Mallory is pretty shrewd, and by all accounts he's damned good at his job. If we're to feed in some false information – see if it comes out the other end, so to speak, we've firstly got to get someone to prepare it who's right on the ball. If we don't Mallory'll smell a rat. But to get someone who's well enough qualified we've got to widen the circle a bit. That lets someone else in on the secret.'

'You can't make an omelette without breaking eggs, Hector, and you're right – if you feed any duff information in, he'll spot it in an instant.'

Toogood nodded gravely. 'I suppose we could wait to see if he actually handed anything over to this woman.'

'Catch him in the act, you mean?'

'Yes.'

Gaffney shook his head. 'Too risky. Suppose we followed him to a meet on the one day he had nothing? That would blow it completely. It would warn him off, and then we'd never get any evidence. What's more they'd have to give him his bloody knighthood. And that would absolutely choke the Prime Minister, from what Carfax was saying.'

'I'll have to speak to the legal adviser about it. I'm sure that to feed something in like that would be regarded as acting as *agent provocateur*.' He paused. 'Wouldn't it?'

'Not unless that was the only evidence you intended to adduce. But in our case it would be a means to an end. It would enable us to interview him – under caution – search his house, his desk, and go over his bank account with a fine toothcomb.'

'Mmm!' Toogood still looked doubtful. 'I think I'd better speak to the LA all the same.'

'There is the little matter of a murder, too,' said Gaffney quietly.

'Do you really think he had anything to do with that, John?'

Gaffney spread his hands. 'In this game, Hector, you never make judgments without evidence – although you do sometimes play hunches. But C1 Branch have been told to lay off until we've finished messing about. But the French won't be too happy with the delay. Trouble is, we can't tell them why we're holding back. Still, I suppose we'll just have to play it by ear, as usual.'

160

'You know we haven't got very much on him, have we? Just one meeting with a South African girl who happens to work at the embassy.'

'A very attractive girl by all accounts,' said Gaffney.

'What's that got to do with it?'

'It could just be a case of *cherchez la femme*. After all, we know for a fact that he was screwing his secretary.'

Toogood swallowed. 'Er – yes, I suppose so.'

A whole fortnight went by. The log of telephone calls made to and from the Mallory's home, and the calls to and from his office telephone, ran into pages. They were closely analysed, but merely confirmed for the most part what the police and the Security Service knew already, that Lady Francesca Mallory was having an affair with Sean Pearce. And was quite happily – and knowingly – sharing him with her daughter. Ironically there was no further evidence of Robert Mallory's infidelity, but Gaffney, with all the cynicism of his trade, knew that it had to come sooner or later – and it did. It was not the telephone log that revealed it, but the surveillance log. On the first occasion it happened the watchers were very nearly caught out.

Leaving the office a little later than usual, they were surprised to see Mallory usher his secretary, Kate McLaren, into his official car. They knew that she lived in Hampstead and presumed that Mallory was dropping her off; not far out of his way home to Chalfont. Nor were they surprised when the car stopped outside a fashionable pub in Hampstead; again the watchers made a presumption – this time that Mallory was buying his hard-working secretary a drink. That seemed quite reasonable a reward for her having worked overtime.

One of the watchers did the nearest thing to a forward roll out of the following vehicle, and nonchalantly strolled into the pub after them. They were not there. But watchers are experienced at their trade, and one of the truisms upon which they work is that if the quarry is not where you think, then clearly it is somewhere else. Abandoning all pretence of discretion, the watcher quickly checked the men's room, working on the assumption that he might be there, and that she equally could be in the ladies. He wasn't.

Quickly he surveyed the inside of the small pub. There was a door at the back. He got outside just in time to see Mallory and Kate McLaren walking swiftly up the small street that met the rear of the pub at right angles. The watcher saw them round a corner and reached the junction just in time to see Kate McLaren putting her key into the door of a flat over a mews garage. Then she and Mallory went inside.

By the time they emerged, an hour later, the watcher had established from control that the flat was Kate McLaren's private address. She and Mallory walked back down the street, in through the door of the pub, and out again through the front door. Then they got into the car and drove off, round by the road, stopping in front of the very flat they had left only minutes previously. Mallory dropped her off without so much as a pecked cheek.

The chauffeur didn't care – he was on overtime. Charlie Markham would have been furious, but he never got to find out.

But nothing turned up to prove that Mallory was a spy, just that he was human – and immoral. John Gaffney looked upon Lady Francesca Mallory in an entirely different light. Good luck to her was his pithy comment.

The next meeting between Toogood and Gaffney was two days later.

'I may have to revise my previous ideas about Mallory and the murder of Penelope Lambert,' said Gaffney.

'Oh?'

'Our enquiries at the Foreign Office – through your contact there – have revealed that Mallory was away from the office for a long weekend in August: Friday

162

to Monday inclusive.' He smiled. 'It was the same week-end that Penelope Lambert was in France – and was murdered.'

'Good Lord! Was it a conference or something? I know he spends time away – EEC stuff, and that sort of thing.'

''Fraid not, Hector. We've checked. He was definitely on leave.'

'Do we know where he went?'

'The address he left was that of a small hotel in Ayrshire. He mentioned to someone that he was spending the week-end golfing.'

'Oh well—'

'But he didn't.'

'You've checked?'

'Naturally,' said Gaffney. 'We are quite professional, you know. Anyway, it's unusual to go on a golfing weekend on your own, I'd have thought. Taking a chance on getting a partner, surely?'

Toogood looked doubtful. 'It's a bit thin, isn't it? There could be all manner of explanations for that. It might just be plain resentment at the Foreign Office needing to know where their senior officials are when they're on leave.'

'Spoken like a true civil servant, Hector. We have to do it all the time.'

'He could have gone anywhere,' said Toogood, reluctant to read anything suspicious into Mallory's week-end away. 'He could have changed his mind at the last minute.'

Gaffney nodded slowly. 'That's possible, but it's a strange coincidence that it's the same weekend as the one on which the attractive Mrs Lambert met her death. And she was his secretary, don't forget.'

'And he was having an affair with her, John. Do you think he's got another woman somewhere?'

'Well we know he has now – Kate McLaren. But it's unlikely that his affair with her started before she came to

163

work for him – which was after Penelope's death, of course. And there's always Eva van Heem.'

'But even so, why should he have murdered her – if he did?'

'That we don't know – not yet.'

'Aren't you assuming rather a lot?' asked Toogood.

'I'm not assuming anything. We know Mallory was away from his office for the same weekend as Penelope Lambert, and that he left an address in Scotland where he was supposedly staying for a golfing holiday, but never arrived.'

'Could have changed his mind at the last moment – or perhaps he didn't make a booking and couldn't get in when he got there. It was August, after all.'

'He didn't— '

'You've checked!' said Toogood resignedly.

'We've checked, yes. Mind you, that's not positive. There are a lot of people milling around in Scotland in August, and the proprietors of the hotel can only say that they turned away a lot of people. They don't remember Mallory.'

'Well then— '

'But the Strathclyde Police have been very thorough – they always are – they've checked every other hotel in a wide area. He didn't stay at any of them.'

'Wasn't that a bit risky?' asked Toogood.

'What?'

'If he gets to hear that enquiries are being made about his holiday arrangements?'

'They weren't.'

Toogood raised an eyebrow but said nothing.

'We're not complete fools,' said Gaffney, but he was smiling as he spoke. 'They said they were looking for someone else, and examined the registers. Police do have the power, you know.'

'Does any of that help? Our case, I mean.'

'Probably not. I've passed it to C1. Not that they can do anything about it at the moment. It must be

164

very frustrating for them – having a murder enquiry they can't get on with. By the way, Hector, is there any chance that your watchers can get a photograph of Mallory?'

'I should think so. Why?'

'I'm trying to do what I can to help the C1 chaps. They've still got three sets of unexplained fingerprints in Penelope Lambert's flat in Wimbledon. Apparently the woman in the flat downstairs is a bit on the nosey side, fortunately. They wanted to try a photograph of Mallory on her – see if she recognised him. It would be useful to know how long their affair had been going on.'

'Well I'm not too sure that we'd want— '

'Save us sending out a nondescript van and photographer, Hector. They might just get in the way of your blokes – and we are investigating a murder, you know.'

'Yes, OK, but not to be used in evidence. We can't have our blokes appearing in court.'

'Oh I know,' said Gaffney with a sigh. 'Yes, indeed – I do know that.'

Harry Tipper accepted the tit-bit that Special Branch had thrown him, and sent Charlie Markham down to Wimbledon.

'It's the police, Mrs Mason – DS Markham – remember me?' Markham always felt rather foolish, conducting a tortuous conversation with a metal box next to a front door, but there was no other way of getting in to see the ballet mistress who kept herself to herself – sometimes.

'I had rather hoped that I'd seen the last of the police,' she said, when eventually Markham had been admitted to her sitting-room. 'Which reminds me – am I to get the keys back?'

'The keys, Mrs Mason?'

'To that poor girl's flat.'

'I'm afraid not. Why do you want them?'

'Well I did undertake to look after the place for her, and now she's dead, well I feel a debt of honour to whoever are her – what d'you call them – next-of-kin?'

Markham smiled. 'I'm afraid you won't be getting the keys back, Mrs Mason.' He was fairly certain that she wanted to have one last rummage around – now that she knew Penelope Lambert was dead, and for no other reason.

'Oh!' She sounded quite disappointed. 'What have you come down for?'

'I'd like you to look at this photograph, Mrs Mason.' The watchers had done a good job. It was an almost full-face shot of Mallory, taken at lunchtime two days previously during one of his habitual walks around St James's Park. It was good. Strolling as though he hadn't a care in the world. It had quite disconcerted Gaffney. Perhaps he hadn't any cares. And it might be that Gaffney was right the first time. He wouldn't have been the first government employee to have an affair with a foreign diplomat, however injudicious it might subsequently turn out to be. Strange how the promise of sex banished all caution from even the shrewdest of men.

'Oh yes,' said Mrs Mason without hesitation. 'He's been here.'

'You're certain?'

'Yes. I just happened to come out of my flat as he was coming down the stairs.'

'I see.' Markham thought that that would have been no coincidence.

'I said "Good evening" – of course— '

'Of course,' murmured Markham.

'And he said that he'd just dropped some papers in for Mrs Lambert. It seemed a funny thing to say.'

'Why's that?'

'Well, it's nothing to do with me who she had calling. After all, they're self-contained flats.'

166

'Yes, I suppose so. And you're quite certain that this was the man?'

'Absolutely – no doubt about it.' Mrs Mason looked intently at the policeman. 'Was poor Mrs Lambert murdered, Sergeant?'

'What on earth makes you think that?'

'Well you police seem to be taking an awful lot of interest in her.'

Markham smiled. 'I think you've been watching too much television, Mrs Mason. The fact is that we are making all these enquiries for the French police. She was drowned in France, you see – and they keep sending lists of questions for us to get answers to. It's all a bit of a nuisance, really.'

'Mmm!' She was clearly not satisfied, and Markham supposed that in her lonely unremarkable life, she really wanted there to be a mystery.

'Sorry not to have a murder for you, Mrs Mason. And thank you very much – you've been most helpful.'

Markham had brought the keys of Penelope Lambert's flat with him, and now opened the front door. There was something he wanted to satisfy himself about. He went into the bedroom and opened the door of the wardrobe. He was disappointed to discover that there was no two-way mirror, and no shelf brackets inside. In a way, though, their absence tended to support the theory that whatever had been her motives, the instigation almost certainly came from the South African, Webster.

Chapter Fourteen

The grizzled head of *Maréchal des Logis-Chef* Gaston Givry appeared round the door. 'You have a moment?'

'What is it, *Chef*?'

'The matter of Mrs Lambert.'

'Ah!' Jules Courbet laid down his pen. The matter of Mrs Lambert was an unsatisfactory one. Ever since the discovery of the young woman's body on the foreshore at St Brouille and the disconcerting announcement by Dr Vernet that she had been murdered – well, that drowning was not the cause of death – the examining magistrate had been plaguing him with demands for progress. Scotland Yard had admittedly identified the girl, but had not helped one little bit in finding her killer. He supposed that they had taken the view that a murder committed in France was a problem for the French. Grudgingly he acknowledged that had the reverse been the case, he too might have been reluctant to get enthusiastic when there were so many other things to be done.

'We have discovered where Mrs Lambert was staying, Captain.'

Courbet nodded, and with delicate movements, replaced the cap of his fountain pen. 'So?'

'Not one hundred metres from where her body was found.'

Courbet looked at the ceiling and back at Givry. 'It is not possible.'

'I have a positive identification, Captain. The Rue de la Digue contains a number of houses, yes?'

'Go on.'

'Some are let out— '

'But we have checked all the *gîtes* and all the *logis*, surely?'

'They are not always *gîtes* or *logis*, Captain. This one – where she was – for instance, was not.'

'Yes, yes. Get on.'

'It was hired by Mrs Lambert through an advertisement in a periodical in England. I have seen the woman who owns it and I have shown her the picture. It is her.'

'How did you find out, *Chef*?'

'I had my men call at every house in St Brouille.'

The Captain scoffed. 'Every house – surely not.'

'Well not every house. We drew up a list of houses that we knew were likely. Showed the photograph around, you know?'

Courbet smiled. 'Good police work, eh?'

Givry inclined his head slightly, acknowledging one of the Captain's rare compliments.

'And yesterday evening— '

'How did you know about the advertisement in the English magazine?' He pointed a manicured forefinger at Givry.

'The woman – a Madame Salbris – told me.'

'Was she alone there, this Mrs Lambert?'

'No, Captain, She was accompanied by a man.'

'Name?'

Givry spread his hands and shrugged. 'Alas, no, Captain. She does not know it.'

Courbet swore. 'A description? Did you get a description?'

Givry opened the folder he had brought with him, and withdrew a piece of paper. 'It is anyone,' he said.

Courbet read through Givry's brief report and tutted. 'As you say, *Chef* – it is anyone or everyone.' He handed back the paper. 'I must telephone Tipper. Perhaps it will provoke him into some action.' He shook his head slowly as if he had just asked the impossible.

'Well it's taken them long enough,' said Tipper.

'When did you hear, sir?' asked Markham.

'Just had a phone call.' Courbet, in common with most policemen throughout the world, knew better than to wait for Interpol, and much of the day to day work of criminal investigation was now done by direct telephone calls.

'Was she there alone?'

'It seems not.' Tipper passed his notes over to Markham. 'But if you can identify anyone out of that, you're welcome to swear out an information.'

'Yeah – well that fits about two-thirds of the blokes walking down Victoria Street right now, I should think. It certainly doesn't positively fit any of the men who've come into the frame so far. What about the photograph of Mallory, guv?'

'What about it?'

'The one I took down to Wimbledon – to Mrs Mason.'

'Yeah, I know.'

'Any chance of sending it over to the French? See if they can get an ident?'

'Nothing to lose,' said Tipper, 'but I'll have to speak to SB about it, see if they'll release it.'

'Why? We've got the bloody thing.'

'I know, Charlie, but Special Branch works in mysterious ways – and they never tell us what they're up to. Bloody secret squirrels. That photograph was given to us specifically to show to Mrs Mason. I'll have to speak to Mr Gaffney before we can send it across the Channel.'

Tipper dialled Detective Chief Superintendent Gaffney's number and put the problem to him. Needless to say, he didn't get an immediate answer.

Gaffney spoke to Hector Toogood at the Security Service, who spoke to his director, before, somewhat reluctantly, the

170

permission was given. The usual caveat was imposed, that no one should reveal where the photograph had come from, and they even asked that the Yard's photographic branch should take out the background in case anyone in Brittany should identify it as St James' Park. For what difference that'll make, Tipper said.

The result was predictable. Givry showed the photograph to Madame Salbris who shrugged and said she wasn't sure. Maybe it was – but again, maybe it wasn't.

Gaffney's reaction was to discount it as of no great importance. His main concern, and that of the Security Service, was to determine whether or not Mallory was spying for South Africa. A French murder enquiry, apparently unconnected, did not come very high in his list of priorities. Tipper's suggestion that he and Markham should travel to France again to further their enquiries was dismissed as unnecessary. Possibly even counter-productive.

Chapter Fifteen

In order to operate successfully, the Security Service needs to have contacts. Such contacts need to be spread wide, and ideally, placed in key appointments in diverse fields. They have to be of proven trustworthiness, and above all, discreet. For most of the time they are dormant, unaware that they are waiting to be used, perhaps for just one operation, or to provide one piece of information. And often too, the one contribution they can make will, on its own, be meaningless to them – a single piece of the jigsaw, as MI5 is so fond of saying.

One such person was Geoffrey Fuller. Now in his early sixties, he had led an infantry platoon onto the beaches of Normandy in 1944, only to be repatriated forty-eight hours later, minus a foot but with a Military Cross; a transaction which in later life he was often to describe as an exchange of dubious advantage.

Since that time he had hobbled around the world, building up an impressive business empire, the wealth of which was founded firmly on import and export. His impeccable concern, which he described deprecatingly as buying and selling, had a reputation of the highest integrity, and apart from the similarity of their operation, had nothing in common with that owned, for example by Richard Jacob, who would unhesitatingly hire a discriminating stripper like Penelope Lambert in order to clinch a deal, giving not a thought to the immorality of it all.

But there are degrees of immorality, and a strong body of public opinion held the view that it was immoral to trade with South Africa. That too was debatable; to withhold trade, said others, was also immoral, because it would be the blacks who would suffer, not the white ruling minority. Geoffrey Fuller closed his eyes to such polemics; he was only a business man.

Such finer points of the political argument did not worry the Security Service too much either, and their real concern was to determine whether a particular man at a particular time would serve their purpose.

But cautiously. The school you had been to, the clubs you belonged to, and the company you kept, all helped officers of MI5 to gauge your probity. Nevertheless, there were ex-public schoolboys to be found in Wormwood Scrubs, and doubtless there was a rogue or two in even the best London clubs – Hector Toogood didn't know; he wasn't a member of any of them.

Consequently a great deal of arcane enquiry work went on, even though Carfax, Toogood's boss, knew Fuller socially, and had put his name forward in the first place.

'Mr Fuller, my name is Granger – Robin Granger,' said Toogood. 'I understand that Mr Gaffney here mentioned that I would be coming to see you.'

'So did John Carfax.' Fuller smiled.

'Ah! Quite so. In that case you've probably guessed what we're here for.'

'No!' Fuller smiled again.

Toogood looked furtive. 'Well . . . '

Fuller decided to help him out. 'Look, old boy, I know you're from Five, and that you want some help – yes?'

'Well, yes, Mr Fuller, that's it exactly.'

'Good. Well fire away.' Fuller sat back in one of the armchairs grouped in the corner of his large office.

'I hope you don't mind the formality,' said Toogood, fumbling in his brief-case, 'but I have to ask you to sign this. It's a declaration under the Official Secrets Act.'

Fuller laughed, took out his pen and scribbled his signature at the foot of the form.

'You really ought to read it, Mr Fuller.'

'I've signed dozens of 'em old boy. I reckon you chaps must have a file of 'em that thick.' He held up his hand, the forefinger and thumb about two inches apart.

'Quite so,' said Toogood again. Gaffney groaned inwardly. He wished to God that he'd get on with it. At last he did, taking what for him was a leap forward into the unknown. 'We have reason to believe that there is a leakage of information from the Foreign Office. It has to do with South Africa.'

'Oh?' Fuller's veneer of flippancy vanished. 'Not to do with this company, I hope.'

'Good Lord no. There's no suggestion— '

'That's a relief.'

'But it's in that direction that we're hoping that you can be of some help to us.'

'I'll certainly do what I can, Mr er – Granger. What did you have in mind?'

'We want to feed in a spurious economic intelligence report to a certain individual at the Foreign Office. Something along the lines that you intend to stop trading with South Africa. That you've had quite enough of threats from people opposed to apartheid – that sort of thing – and they've hinted that they'll disrupt your business.'

Fuller looked doubtful. 'What's the point of that?'

'We suspect that information of that sort is being passed to the South African government. The advantage to the South Africans of receiving it in advance of its happening will be obvious to you. Particularly in the field of their manufacturing industries – such as they are.'

Fuller held up a staying hand. 'Just a moment. I do quite a lot of business with South Africa. Now whatever

174

the moral implications of that happen to be is neither here nor there. But if that sort of information gets passed to the South Africans it really could damage my business.'

'There is no intention that it will, Mr Fuller. The report will be strictly controlled— '

'But you said that it could be passed to the South African Government— '

'Yes, but it won't reach them. We'll make sure of that.'

'How can you be so certain?'

'I'm as certain as can be. You see we are pretty sure that we know how the information is passed, and we'll be in a position to stop it.'

'And what then do you want me to do?'

'It is essential that this information has the ring of truth about it. It may be that our . . . ' He hesitated. 'It may be that our suspect will contact you, to verify that what he has been told is true, although I doubt it. But it would be quite legitimate for him to do so. That, after all, is what he is there for.'

'What precisely is he there for?'

'The collation of economic reports – among a wide variety of other things – that will assist HMG to formulate its foreign trading policies.'

'Very well, then – although I must admit I'm not awfully happy about it . . . Incidentally, what is the name of the man concerned?'

'I'm afraid that I cannot reveal that, Mr Fuller.'

'Then how the hell am I supposed to know if he rings me?'

Toogood smiled patiently. 'There is only one man who will ring you, Mr Fuller – the only man who'll have the information. I doubt if he'll identify himself, but if he does, then so be it.'

'Seems a damned funny way of doing things,' growled Fuller.

There are some very clever men in the Security Service, men who are experts in all manner of specialised and

175

unusual fields. One of their economists prepared a very clever report setting out Mr Fuller's reservations about continuing to trade with South Africa, and adding that he intended to stop doing so.

There was some debate about what security classification should be put on this document. 'Top Secret' was vetoed on the grounds that it manifestly was not top secret; 'Secret' was bandied about a bit, but similarly dismissed because it was out of character for a document of that calibre, and, as there was no source disclosed, there was none to protect. Finally they settled for the all-embracing 'Confidential'. Attribution of the report was not revealed, but a smart little phrase, familiar in government circles, implied that it had come from the Security Service itself. Toogood thought that to be quite amusing.

The watchers did not have long to wait. There were no telephone calls arranging a meeting, but that was no surprise. However, Eva van Heem received a catalogue for a washing-machine through the post. The Security Service was as sure as possible that she had not requested a catalogue for a washing-machine, and in any event the envelope had been handwritten and posted in central London – nowhere near the offices or the factory of the manufacturers, who were based in the north.

Toogood, familiar with the ways of espionage, and conversant with many case histories, knew the signs, and put the watchers on extra alert. He was sure that there was going to be a meet – but he didn't know where.

Three surveillance teams were mobilised. One in the vicinity of Eva van Heem's home in Hendon, another at Chalfont St Giles and, for good measure, a third in the vicinity of the pub at Mornington Crescent. Each team consisted of Security Service and Special Branch officers.

Miss van Heem emerged from the South African Embassy at exactly half-past twelve and made her way directly to the Underground station at Embankment. The watchers swore; personal radios do not work effectively on the Underground.

Robert Mallory emerged from the Foreign Office, also at half-past twelve, and ambled along King Charles Street. Down the Clive Steps he went, across Horse Guards Approach Road and into the park. The team watching him were certain that a devious plan was about to unfold.

Eva van Heem waited while a Richmond train came in and left. Then a Wimbledon train arrived which she boarded at the last moment just before the doors closed. Clear evidence, three of the watchers thought, of some training in counter-surveillance techniques. That view was confirmed when she alighted at Earls Court, a station at which the previous train had also stopped. The watchers made every effort to inform their control, but transmission was impossible until one of their number ascended to street level and told the team watching Mallory what was going on. He was interested to learn that so far Mallory hadn't made a move – was still watching the birds in St James's Park. By the time that that watcher got back to the platform his colleagues and Miss van Heem had disappeared. Again he tried to transmit – again without success.

The watchers who had stayed with Eva van Heem were now trapped. She had shot on to a Piccadilly Line train, again waiting until the last moment, and they too had had no option but to follow. But they couldn't tell anyone.

The team at Mornington Crescent were beginning to feel left out. They had heard the transmissions of the Mallory team when they had announced that they were taking him to the park – as usual, one watcher laconically announced. And then they had heard the hurried report of Eva's arrival at Earls Court – and then nothing.

'I don't know what the hell's happening,' said Toogood. He was sitting in the control room at the Security Service head-quarters, Gaffney alongside him. Each had his own concern about the operation. Toogood to monitor the movements of the prime suspects; only too well aware that one of them was a diplomat. Gaffney, anxious that when the time came to make an arrest, his men should be in the right place and, more important, that there should be sufficient evidence to justify the arrest that they were to make, particularly as someone with diplomatic immunity was involved. In his mind, Gaffney ran over the points that would have to be covered in the report for the Home Secretary, points that would give the Foreign Secretary adequate grounds for declaring Eva van Heem *persona non grata* – with all the questions that would follow in the House. It was an anxiety shared by Toogood, who knew only too well that criticism would inevitably be made of his service. It was one of the great injustices; the Security Service would be praised for discovering a spy and at once pilloried for failing to have done so much sooner. He could see already the judge at the Old Bailey condemning in censorious terms 'the grave damage' that had been done to the nation – and so on, and so on.

One of the controllers turned to face Toogood, his ear-phones still in position lest he should miss something vital. 'She's alighted at Heathrow Airport, sir.'

'Oh, Christ,' said Toogood. 'Don't tell me she's going home.'

The controller swung around again. 'She's walking through Terminal Two, sir.'

'What's she doing? Does it look as though she's going somewhere?'

The controller laughed. 'She's just gone into the loo.'

Toogood pouted. 'I hope to God they've got a woman on the team.'

'They have,' said Gaffney. 'One of ours.'

There were in fact eleven women on the team – eleven out of a total of thirty watchers. The Security Service always had adequate reserves for a big operation, working on the theory that if there wasn't a crowd, make your own. It seemed crazy to the uninitiated, but bitter experience had taught them that it was a sure way of alleviating suspicion. Not that they had to worry at Heathrow where there were crowds enough – always.

One of the women watchers glanced in the mirror over the washhand basin as Eva van Heem emerged from one of the cubicles. Quickly she switched on the electric hand-dryer to drown her transmission and spoke a single word into the microphone in her cuff, 'Moving.'

The constant traffic of aircraft, and the continuous exchange of chatter between pilots and control tower made transmissions difficult enough between even the watchers in close proximity to one another at the airport. To talk to those following Mallory was impossible.

'It's the usual bloody cock-up,' said one of the watchers bitterly.

Suddenly it happened. Eva van Heem walked towards the tall good-looking man near the bookstall. They brushed past each other, almost casually, and any but the dedicated onlooker would have missed the magazine that passed between them.

'Right – move in – take them both.' Detective Chief Inspector Terry Dobbs spoke quietly into the handset attached to his wrist. The MI5 watchers stayed back as the Special Branch officers closed in; four went for the girl – three of them women; and another four, all men, surrounded the man who had handed her the periodical.

'What is this? What's happening? Help me – I'm being robbed.' There was no mistaking the Afrikaans accent.

'We're police officers,' said Detective Sergeant Claire Wentworth as her colleagues sought to restrain the struggling diplomat.

'Get your hands off me – I'm a diplomat. I have diplomatic status,' said the South African.

'They all say that,' said Claire Wentworth.

By contrast, the man held by police some ten yards distant put up no opposition, but stood docile and resigned as Detective Chief Inspector Dobbs cautioned him.

One of the watchers telephoned Toogood in control. 'We've got them both, sir,' he said.

'Both?'

'Yes – van Heem and Mallory.'

'You haven't, you know. Mallory returned to his office ten minutes ago.'

Chapter Sixteen

Attractive woman though she was, there was no doubt that Eva van Heem was a hard-bitten professional. Once it was made clear to her that she had been detained by real police officers and wasn't the victim of an attack, she had remained absolutely silent, for most of the time a cynical smile on her face.

She and her male contact were conveyed separately to Heathrow Airport Police Station and there detained in separate interview rooms.

One of the levelling aspects of British police practice is that no matter how serious the crime alleged against a prisoner, it is a sergeant who deals with him or her when first they arrive at a police station. The sergeant – called a custody officer – who was on duty at the time the two alleged spies were brought in, was a man of fifty-one years of age. He had a house in Pinner, a wife, two daughters and a dog, all of whom – at least the humans – accused him of devoting more time to his garden than to them.

'Now then,' he said, settling himself at his desk. 'Just give me your full name, address and date of birth – that'll do for a start.'

'I am Eva van Heem, a second secretary at the South African Embassy. I am entitled to diplomatic privilege. I refuse to answer any questions, and I demand that I be released immediately.'

'Well now,' said the Sergeant with a smile. 'We'll have to see. You appreciate, of course, that anyone can say that, so I'll have to do some checking.'

'Be quick about it, man, or your superiors will hear about the delay.' She was starting to show signs of anger.

The Sergeant smiled as he lumbered to his feet. 'I've no doubt they'll be hearing about it anyway, miss.'

They already knew of course. The Security Service knew. The Special Branch knew, and in the time it had taken Eva van Heem to reach Heathrow Airport Police Station, the Foreign Secretary, the Home Secretary and the Commissioner of Police had been informed. And they all knew what would happen next.

'I must apologise for your having been detained, madam,' said Detective Chief Superintendent John Gaffney who had arrived seconds earlier from Security Service headquarters, the keening siren of his police car carving a priority passage for him through the early afternoon M4 traffic. 'You will, of course, be released straight away. I have arranged for a car to take you to the embassy. Incidentally, I have taken the liberty of informing your ambassador.' Gaffney smiled a wintry smile. 'He may have been worried about you.'

Eva van Heem scowled. 'You realise, I hope, that there will be an official note of protest about this – at the highest level.'

'I have no doubt, madam,' murmured Gaffney.

And so Eva van Heem left the airport to return to her embassy. Within twenty-four hours she was back again, to board a flight bound for Johannesburg, before Her Majesty's Government had even declared her *persona non grata*. There was no protest. Not even a formal one.

In the other interview room at Heathrow Airport Police Station, John Wallace sat disconsolately, head bowed, hands between his knees. John Gaffney sat down opposite him.

182

Toogood sat in a corner, trying to pretend that he was invisible.

'You're not obliged to say anything unless you wish to do so,' said Gaffney, 'but anything you do say will be taken down in writing and may be given in evidence.'

'They told me that already,' said Wallace miserably.

'I know,' said Gaffney. 'I just want to make sure that you're under no illusions as to your position.'

'Aren't you supposed to ask me if I want a solicitor?'

'No,' said Gaffney, 'but you can ask me for one. I shouldn't bother though. If I decide that it is likely to interfere with my enquiries into an Official Secrets Act case, the answer will be no – is in fact no.'

He opened a file and withdrew a piece of paper enclosed now in a plastic sleeve. He laid it on the desk, turning it so that Wallace could see it. 'This is the report which was secreted in the magazine that you passed to Miss van Heem. It is an official government report and it is classified Confidential.' Wallace nodded. 'Where did you get it from?'

'It was sent to me.'

'How?'

'Through IDS – the internal despatch service.'

'Who sent it?'

'Mr Mallory at the Foreign Office.'

'Why should he do a thing like that?'

'He often sends me things like that. We tend to overlap in our jobs. He has something to do with economic affairs at the FCO, and I deal with them from a Department of Trade angle.'

'Did he know that you were going to pass it to a second secretary at the South African Embassy?'

A fleeting, weary smile crossed Wallace's face. 'Christ no!'

At that moment one of the detectives from Gaffney's team came into the room and laid a thick file of papers on the desk. Gaffney looked up, a frown on his face. He disliked being interrupted in the middle of an interrogation

– it often broke the spell. 'What's that?' he asked crossly.

'They've just been brought down from the office, sir. Mr Dobbs said you'd probably need to have them by you.'

Gaffney glanced at the cover. It was the docket on the enquiries into the death of Penelope Lambert. 'Ah, yes, indeed,' he said. 'Thank you.' And turning his attention once more to Wallace, 'Why were you passing information of this sort to Eva van Heem?'

Wallace hesitated. He knew he was in deep trouble. 'I've got nothing to say.'

Gaffney took out a packet of cigarettes. 'D'you smoke?' He extended the packet towards the prisoner.

'Thank you.' Wallace took one hungrily, waiting for Gaffney to produce his lighter.

'Good-looking woman – Miss van Heem, isn't she?'

Wallace blew smoke into the air and nodded. 'Yes.'

The atmosphere in the tiny room was starting to get oppressive. The only windows were narrow, with wired, frosted glass, and were near to the ceiling. Both were open to their limit – only a few inches. It suited Gaffney; he was accustomed to such working conditions – Wallace was not.

'If you are trying to defend Eva out of some misplaced sense of chivalry, Mr Wallace, I shouldn't bother. She has certainly not done so for you.'

In fact, Eva van Heem hadn't done anything; had said nothing that would either implicate or excuse what Wallace was accused of, but it was essential that Gaffney drove a divide between the two conspirators if he was to get the answers to all the Security Service's questions. The trial and conviction of Wallace was now of little importance, superseded by the need to estimate what damage had been done. Fortunately it did not appear too serious, at least not so far. The question of trade economics, important though it was, did not feature too highly in the general scheme of things. The worrying doubt that the Security Service, and, in turn, the government now had was that of military deployment.

184

How far had the cancer spread? If full–scale revolution were to break out in South Africa, certain contingency plans had been made, to deal with it, certain secret treaties entered into, all of which could be highly damaging if released prematurely.

'What will happen to Eva?' asked Wallace.

'Absolutely nothing,' said Gaffney. 'The worst will be that the British government declares her *persona non grata* and she'll be sent back to South Africa, no doubt to a heroine's welcome, before being sent off somewhere else to dupe some other poor fool into parting with his country's secrets.' He leaned back, allowing time for that significant statement to sink in.

Wallace sat silent, refusing to meet the policeman's gaze. Eventually he looked up. 'She's screwed me, hasn't she?'

Gaffney refrained from making the obvious retort; this was not an occasion for clever remarks. 'It looks very much like it.' He waited – waited for Wallace to adjust himself to the concept that he was about to make a full confession. 'How about beginning at the beginning?'

Wallace plunged straight in. 'I got this telephone call one day – at the office. I don't know how she found my number, but she did. She's got a very husky voice – sexy really – I don't know if you noticed.' Gaffney said nothing; but he had noticed. 'I almost laughed because it sounded just like something off the television: "You don't know me, but I know you", is what she said.' He shook his head, briefly, as though wondering now how he had been taken in. 'She suggested that we met somewhere. She had something that was of vital importance to me, is how she put it, and she warned me not to tell a soul, particularly anyone in the department – at least not until after we'd met; then I could make up my own mind, she said.'

'Did she identify herself? Tell you who she was?'

'No – not really. She told me her name was Eva, that was all. We had this silly conversation about how I would know her. I suggested the way they do it in spy novels, you know; holding a copy of *Time Out* with a red rose between my teeth under the clock at Waterloo Station.' He paused reflectively, and pointed at Gaffney's packet of cigarettes. The detective nodded, not wishing to interrupt the flow.

For some time Wallace sat in silence, enjoying the cigarette, detached – his mind elsewhere, as though realising the importance of getting his story absolutely right.

'She said it was serious – not funny at all. To be frank, up until then I'd thought it was someone in the office, having a joke.'

'Go on.'

'She said she would know me, and that I was to go to a pub in Mornington Crescent, get a drink and sit down at a table and wait.'

'And is that what you did?'

'Yes. I went up there after work – straight after work. I was there by about twenty-to-six. She said she'd meet me at six. I told Linda – that's my wife – that I was having to work late at the office— '

'Doesn't she work at the Department of Trade as well?'

'Yes, but in a different section – a different building, in fact. We don't often travel home together anyway, and she's quite used to me having to work late sometimes.'

'Yes.'

'I'd been there about ten minutes when she arrived. She was early too. I still thought it was a joke. I was waiting for half the office to turn up, with a stripagram girl, or something of that sort.'

'Why? Was there any reason? I mean, was it your birthday or anything like that?'

'No, nothing like that. As a matter of fact, I did wonder if Penny might be at the back of it – she's got a weird sense of fun.'

'Penny?'

'Penny Lambert – but you know about that, I suppose?'

'Yes, I do. We'll come back to that later.'

'Well this girl came in. Good figure and quite tall – well, tall for a girl. She was dressed in white jeans, very tight – and a blue sweater. Raised a few eyebrows in that pub, I can tell you. And very confident. Walked up to the bar and got herself a drink. Then she looked round, casually, and came straight over to my table. Believe me, I thought my luck was in – it wasn't though, was it?'

Gaffney declined to commit himself. 'Go on,' he said.

'That's when it started to get nasty. I couldn't believe it at first. She was very cool – very matter-of-fact, and she had this husky voice, like I said. She said her name was Eva – that was all; she didn't tell me her surname. And she said that she knew all about me. It was frightening – she did know all about me. She started talking about my job, and my wife. She knew her name and where we lived, and she knew what I did – in the Department I mean. Then she started talking about Penny.' Again Wallace relapsed into silence, staring into space, as though unable to believe that it was all happening to him – had happened.

'What about Penny?' Gaffney prompted him gently.

'She knew I was still seeing her, and she told me that she was a photographer's model in her spare time, and that she was a stripper.' He shook his head, unbelievingly.

'You sound surprised.' Gaffney paid a silent and grudging tribute to the thoroughness of the South African security machine. He was now certain that Webster, Penny's neighbour at Mexico Road, had been part of that machine.

Wallace looked up, as if bewildered to see the policeman there, intruding on his spoken thoughts. 'Well no, I suppose not really. I'd often wondered about some of the photographic work she did. I was a bit suspicious that she might have been doing the odd provocative pose – not exactly Page Three stuff, that would be too public, particularly as she was working at the Foreign Office, but more private stuff. Anyway this Eva told me that she would sometimes go to very select private parties and do a strip – and she hinted that she might do other things as well. That made me pretty mad, I can tell you. I was almost tempted to slap her face. And she could see I was annoyed too, but she just smiled. The bloody woman just sat there and smiled.'

Gaffney had been flicking through the murder docket as Wallace had been talking, and finding the place, looked up. 'But you knew she did poses of that sort – you took some of her yourself.'

'But that was different – that was private, just for me.'

Gaffney was always mildly amused when people took him for a fool. Wallace had lived with Penelope Lambert for six months and had continued the affair after his own marriage. If he didn't know what she was up to he was deliberately closing his eyes to it. But he did. His statements to Harry Tipper were open in front of Gaffney at this very moment, and the video tapes confirmed that the affair had continued. It was almost certain that Eva van Heem had given him a copy of the one in which he starred.

'Then she spelt it out,' Wallace went on. 'She suggested that I could help her. She said she was connected with the Anti-Apartheid movement, and that they were very concerned about what would happen to the blacks if sanctions were imposed. I told her there was no chance of my doing anything like that, but then she asked me, very quietly – the pub was starting to fill up – what the Department would think if they found out that I was seeing Penny, and if they found out that she was nothing more than a high-class prostitute. And what would my wife think? Then she went on to tell me what I knew already. That I was in debt, and that I couldn't afford to lose my job. I was stunned. Nothing had ever happened to me like that before.'

'And?'

'She didn't say anything for a bit. Well actually she got up and went to the bar – bought some more drinks. She didn't ask me what I wanted – just got me a large Scotch.

I suppose she thought I needed it after that.' He looked straight at Gaffney. 'She's a very strong-willed woman, you know. Used to getting her own way.'

'Obviously,' murmured Gaffney.

'Course she tried to sweeten the pill a bit. She said that they wouldn't be ungrateful; there were quite a few people – people of influence and wealth – who would like to see the South African government brought down, and that they would be quite prepared to pay.'

'What happened then?'

'I told her I didn't believe her – about Penny, I mean. So she told me about a specific party that Penny'd been to – someone called— ' He stopped, searching his memory. 'Jacob – that was it – Richard or Reginald, some name like that; and she said why didn't I ring this bloke up and ask him – or ask Penny.'

'And did you?'

'Yes,' said Wallace miserably. 'And I wished I hadn't.'

'You mean you rang up this Jacob man?'

'Oh Christ no. No, I had it out with Penny.'

'And?'

'She admitted it.' He sounded incredulous, even now. 'She bloody well admitted it. She said it was none of my business if she wanted to take all her clothes off and pose nude for men to take photographs – or do anything else they wanted. I didn't really believe her – I think she was just saying it to annoy me. But she said she wasn't married to me, and if I wanted to have a say in what she did, then perhaps I ought to give her some money, so she wouldn't have to do things like that. Well she knew I couldn't afford that, and like I said, we had a terrible row – that nosey bloody woman downstairs must have heard it.'

'And that was that, presumably?'

'Yes it was. I slapped her face – and she slapped mine. Then I left, and I never saw her again. And now she's dead.'

The last few words were almost lost as Wallace buried his face in his hands and started to sob violently.

Gaffney sat back and waited for him to regain his composure, or stop acting – he wasn't sure which. He lit a cigarette, fighting back the contempt he felt for this immoral and unsavoury little man opposite: not little physically; he was well-built – a squash player he'd said, the kind of macho image the Wallaces of this world tried to create – but insignificant, fighting all his life to be a somebody, when in fact he was a nobody. Until now. If nothing else he would hold centre stage at the Old Bailey for a day or two, before disappearing, once more, into obscurity.

'And so you co-operated.' It was not a question, but Wallace took it as such.

'Yes. What option did I have?' He looked up, seeking acquiescence in the other's face; there was no sign of it.

Gaffney could have told him, as he could have told so many before him, that both the Security Service and Special Branch would have been sympathetic to the blackmail that so often forms a part of the dirty world of espionage. They would have handled it, monitored it, and his wife, his girl-friend, and possibly even his career, would have been untouched by it. But it was always too late. They never believed it. He glanced across at Wallace; he probably wouldn't have believed it, even now.

'What you have been telling me has been tape-recorded,' said Gaffney, 'and a statement will be prepared from the transcription which you will be able to read. You will be able to alter anything you wish, or add to it, and I shall expect you to sign it.' That would make it nice and neat; Gaffney didn't bother to tell him that it didn't matter, whether he signed it. 'Then I shall want another statement from you.' He glanced across at Toogood, still sitting silently in the corner. 'Another statement which will list exactly what you have passed over to Eva van Heem.' He paused as a thought occurred to him. 'Did you ever

190

have any dealings with anyone else – anybody other than van Heem?'

'No.' Wallace shook his head resignedly. 'I don't know about Mallory though.'

Toogood was suddenly jerked out of his reverie. 'Mallory? What about Mallory?'

Gaffney flashed a sharp look of annoyance at the Security Service officer. It said that if he wanted to take part he must be prepared to give evidence at the trial.

Toogood held up a placatory hand. 'Sorry,' he whispered, as though trying to erase his outburst.

'Well? What about Mallory?' Gaffney repeated Toogood's question.

'Eva van Heem wanted to know about him.'

Gaffney leaned back in his chair with a sigh, glanced at the ceiling and folded his arms. Then he levelled his gaze onto Wallace's face. 'What did she want to know?'

'This was some time later. About our third meeting, I suppose. She asked me if I knew a chap called Mallory at the Foreign Office.'

'And did you?'

'Yes, of course. I told you. I get stuff from him from time to time – that for instance.' He pointed at the report which still lay on the table.

Gaffney could have said that he was just testing but he said nothing; it was never a bad idea to let the opposition think that you weren't too bright. 'Why did she want to know about Mallory?'

'I suppose – thinking back on it – that she probably wanted to try the same routine on him as she'd done on me. She knew that Penny was his secretary, for instance – which is more than I knew, at least at the time. And then she asked if I knew that Penny was having an affair with him.'

'And was she?'

'I don't know. After our row, I'd've believed anything of

her, but I didn't see her again, so I couldn't ask her – didn't care by then to be perfectly honest.'

'What happened? D'you know?'

'No.'

'What did you tell her about him?'

'Nothing. There wasn't anything I could say. I really only knew of him by reputation. I'd spoken to him a few times on the telephone, but that was all. I've never even met the bloke.'

'I don't believe you,' said Gaffney. 'In fact, I suggest to you that you were actively involved in blackmailing Mallory, together with Penny.' Wallace remained silent. 'And Jimmy Webster.'

'Webster? Who's Webster? I've never heard of him.'

Strangely enough, Gaffney believed that.

Chapter Seventeen

Gaffney's small office at New Scotland Yard was crowded. Apart from Toogood, there was the desk officer, Charles Monk, John Andrews – the leader of the watchers, and Harry Tipper. Sitting on an upright chair awkwardly placed at the corner of Gaffney's desk, was Terry Dobbs, the Detective Chief Inspector who had arrested Wallace at the airport.

'It's really a question of what we do next,' said Gaffney.

Toogood looked nervously at Tipper; he was always unhappy about the presence of people who had not been positively vetted, as though that process cloaked them with a magical integrity. 'I'm still not very sanguine about Mallory,' he said.

'Neither am I,' said Tipper. 'I still think he's got to be a front-runner for my job.'

'Front-runner?' Toogood looked puzzled.

'Prime suspect for the Lambert murder.' Gaffney translated for him.

'Oh, I see. Well I think that we should deal with our aspect of the matter first.'

'Which is what?' asked Tipper. 'After all, murder is still regarded as a fairly serious matter – even these days.'

'As far as I can see,' said Gaffney, acting as middleman, 'the evidence against Mallory is not very strong, either for the murder or for our OSA job.'

'But he did meet Eva van Heem,' said Monk. He

spoke in an apologetic tone, as though sorry that he had to mention it.

'That's true,' said Toogood. 'And we still don't know why. The only supportable theory so far is that Wallace got the impression that van Heem was trying to enmesh him as she had apparently trapped Wallace himself.'

'She may have succeeded,' said Terry Dobbs. 'We do know that he's having an affair with Kate McLaren.'

'His secretary? I didn't know that,' said Tipper.

Toogood shot a nervous glance at Gaffney.

'It came out of the observation,' said Gaffney, impatient with Toogood's constant concern about protecting his sources.

Toogood was not prepared to let it all go. 'We only know that he went to her flat on a couple of occasions.'

'And stayed an hour,' Gaffney reminded him.

'But that doesn't mean that— '

'A judge once said that if the opportunity for adultery could be proved, it's presumed to have occurred,' said Tipper with a rare flash of legal knowledge.

Gaffney laughed. 'Quite right, Harry. But you won't get a warrant on the strength of it.' He looked round at the others. 'But it still doesn't help us to determine what to do next.' He was always impatient with conferences; they rarely achieved anything – in his experience, anyhow.

'There doesn't seem to be much point in maintaining the surveillance,' said Toogood. 'Wallace's arrest – and more to the point Eva van Heem's – will be in the papers tomorrow morning.'

'It'll be in this evening's,' said Gaffney unhelpfully. 'He was at court this morning.'

'Well, yes – of course. Either way it's going to put Mallory on the alert – make him much more difficult to follow. Frankly, I don't see that there would be much profit in it anyway.'

194

'He might panic – do something out of character,' said Dobbs.

'But what? What can he do? I think he'll probably lie low. He must be reckoning – if he has committed an OSA offence – that if we'd had anything on him, he'd have been arrested at the same time. He must have assumed that he's safe.'

'If he's done anything at all.' Gaffney had had dealings with the Security Service many times before, and he always had to keep pulling them back to earth. Policemen tried to make molehills out of mountains – not the other way round. 'So we take the surveillance off – yes?'

There had been another half-hour of desultory discussion before the conference had decided to discontinue the observation on Mallory. They also decided, somewhat reluctantly, that he should be interviewed, but none of those present had been very optimistic about the result. Mallory was known to be a self-confident, pompous, and rather over-bearing individual. Gaffney was able to deal with people like that, but was experienced enough to know that little was likely to be obtained from them. Dobbs had pointed out that Mallory would have to be seen in any event, to furnish a statement proving that the report that had been passed to Eva van Heem was the one that he had sent to Wallace. It was unlikely that the Director of Public Prosecutions would allow it to be put in evidence, but it was necessary and a quite legitimate device for getting to see Mallory.

'A most unfortunate business,' said Mallory. 'A great shock too, when I read it in the paper – first I knew of it, of course.'

'You knew Wallace well?' asked Gaffney.

'Oh hardly at all – never met the fellow. Of course, he was only a principal, but it was expedient to pass stuff to him direct. Just goes to show, doesn't it?'

'Goes to show what?'

'That you never know. I suppose that's why we're so much more selective in the Foreign Office . . . '

Gaffney felt like deflating this arrogant functionary by mentioning people such as Burgess and MacLean. 'I suppose so,' he said. He took the report in its plastic sleeve, out of his brief-case and laid it on the desk just out of reach. 'Perhaps you'd look at this, Mr Mallory, and tell me if this is the document you passed to Wallace.'

Mallory extended an elegant and manicured hand to draw the report closer. He studied it for some moments before looking up. 'Exactly so,' he said. 'Or perhaps I should say, it appears to be identical. That's the sort of statement you police chaps like, isn't it?'

'More or less,' said Gaffney casually. 'If we haven't got it right, the DPP will soon tell us, and then we'll take another statement. You realise, of course, that it's what you say in court that's important.' He waved a dismissive hand across the desk. 'A statement is taken to give the prosecuting counsel some idea of what you are able to say – it's not evidence in itself, at least not in a case of this magnitude.'

'Yes, of course. I did know that, Superintendent,' said Mallory patronisingly.

Gaffney let that pass, too. The demotion that Mallory had accorded him was unimportant set against what he was trying to achieve. 'Did you ever meet Eva van Heem, incidentally?'

There was not a trace of reaction, not a flicker of emotion on Mallory's face as he answered. 'Who?'

'Eva van Heem – the South African diplomat who was detained when Wallace was arrested.'

'Oh – her. Good Lord no. There would have been no occasion, and, of course, contact with the South Africans is discouraged – quite actively discouraged. It would be most unwise for anybody in the Foreign Office to . . . ' He allowed the statement to wane unfinished.

196

'I'll need to include that in your statement, too,' said Gaffney, pushing a little further, just to see what happened.

'Whatever you wish.'

For several hours that afternoon, Gaffney sat in his office reading through the papers in the case of The Crown *v.* Wallace, and also the docket on the enquiries which had been made about the death of Penelope Lambert, otherwise Gaston – which, he noted, a search at the General Register Office had proved, unsurprisingly, to be her maiden name.

Then he made a telephone call.

The call came to fruition twenty-four hours later with the arrival in his office of the senior fingerprint officer.

'Well, Sid?'

'We've scored, sir – you were right. There are only two sets of fingerprints on the plastic sleeve: yours and Mallory's. His – Mallory's – also appear among several sets on the report itself, and Wallace's of course.'

'Well go on.'

'And Mallory's match the fingermarks on the letter of resignation, in the flat . . . ' He paused dramatically. 'And the partial on the camera.'

'Ah!' Gaffney leaned back in his chair and smiled. 'Well, well. Now there's a thing.'

'Mind you,' said the fingerprint officer cautiously, 'it's not proof. Until we obtain a formal set of prints from Mallory I can't swear to it. Incidentally, what made you put a new plastic sleeve on the exhibit before you went to see him?'

'I don't know really. Just thought it would be a useful thing to do – to acquire a set of his dabs. I'd actually forgotten I'd done it until I came back here and was going through the murder papers. All those unaccounted-for marks in her flat worried me, and then I remembered. Thought I'd give it a run.'

'Well it's a good thing you did, guv'nor. You came up trumps. What are you going to do now?'

'Have another bloody conference, I suppose,' said Gaffney.

Gaffney had decided to restrict the conference this time. Just Hector Toogood and Harry Tipper were in his office. He had invited only the two of them on the grounds that more would be achieved by fewer people.

Harry Tipper, with more practical experience of murder enquiries than the Special Branch Chief Superintendent was pessimistic. 'I agree that he's got some explaining to do, sir,' he said to Gaffney, 'but it doesn't prove that he was Penelope Lambert's killer. He may have a plausible explanation. What have we got? Firstly, his dabs on the letter of resignation.' He started to count the points off on his fingers. 'There could be an acceptable explanation for that. I know he said he'd never seen the letter, but he could withdraw that – say he'd forgotten or something. That doesn't prove he murdered her in France. Then there are the marks in the flat. Well . . . ' There was doubt in his voice. 'We know he was having an affair with the Lambert woman, but he's never denied it, because it's never been put to him, but denying it would be understandable. After all, he's having an affair with Kate McLaren – so your people say.' He glanced at Toogood, who nodded.

'But what about the mark on the camera?' asked Gaffney.

'Even if you accept it is his mark – and Sid said he couldn't prove it – not formally anyway, there is nothing to indicate that it was there after the murder. It's what is called portable evidence.' He paused. 'I'm sorry, sir,' he said to Gaffney, 'I didn't mean to— '

Gaffney smiled. 'It's all right, Harry – I've never investigated a murder, not a conventional one, anyway. Go on.'

'You see,' continued Tipper, 'he could claim that he had

198

loaded the camera – or unloaded it – at her flat, months previously. He could even say that she had brought it to the office one day and asked him to change the film. The helpless woman bit. And from what we know of him, he probably would say that. He's a pretty cool customer. The only thing at the moment is his so far unexplained absence from the office during the same weekend that she was away. Even so, he might come up with a good excuse. Just because he told them he was going golfing in Scotland doesn't mean that he had to. For all we know he might have been having it off with some other bird in the West Country or wherever. It's no crime – it might be a breach of Foreign Office regulations not to tell them where you're going for the weekend – but it won't get you as far as the Bailey.'

'I must say you're a great comfort, Harry.'

'Well, you've got to look at all the possible defences this bloke'll put up, guv'nor. He's pretty shrewd – I don't reckon you'll get a cough out of him on the strength of what we've got so far. Anyway, the Director'd never let it go to court – not on the basis of his fifty per cent rule.'

Gaffney nodded. He knew about the Director of Public Prosecutions' distaste for taking cases to court that had a less than evens chance of succeeding. 'But let's put it all together for a moment, Harry. What you've got, and what Hector and I have got. There's a danger here, if we're not careful, of dealing with the two jobs in isolation. Firstly, he denies ever having met Eva van Heem. We know that's a lie – the C11 surveillance team can put him in a pub in Mornington Crescent with her. That's what started it all. Secondly, there are the marks in the flat, on the letter, and on the camera – and I accept all you say about that, but leave it for a minute; and thirdly, there's his weekend or whatever, allegedly in Scotland, where pretty certainly, he wasn't. And then there's— '

'I've just had a thought, sir,' said Tipper, interrupting. 'Sorry, but it just occurred to me.'

199

'Yes?'

'Suppose he did go to France with Penelope Lambert. Set aside the murder for a moment – just suppose it was a dirty weekend.' He chuckled. 'They go off for a cosy couple of days in a French bed. No thought of murder – that doesn't matter for the moment. Now Mr Toogood here says that Mallory was in the running for a knighthood, which is apparently very important to people like him. Presumably he wouldn't want to upset his chances by being caught having it off with his secretary in France.' Tipper paused before saying, triumphantly, 'So he wouldn't use his own passport, would he? He'd be afraid that the French immigration checks would show it up. You know how they work. The local Old Bill come round and collect up the cards, and he'd be on permanent record. Now he wouldn't like that; he's in the Foreign Office – he knows how these things work.'

'It's a good point, Harry, but didn't you ask the French police if they'd done checks on that – after they discovered where Mrs Lambert had been staying?'

Tipper nodded slowly. 'Yes, you're right, I did.'

'And what did they say?'

Tipper laughed sarcastically. 'There was no trace of either of them; neither Penelope Lambert nor the bloke who was with her.'

'So much for that, then.'

'You'll be pleased to learn, sir, that the French police are going to prosecute the owner of the house for failing to have cards filled in and forwarded to the proper authority.'

'Big deal,' said Gaffney.

'But Mallory – if it's Mallory we're talking about – wasn't to know in advance that that was going to happen. He couldn't have afforded to take a chance on it. I still say he wouldn't have used his own passport.'

'What then?'

'BVP,' said Tipper.

'What's a BVP?' asked Toogood.

'British Visitors Passport,' said both policemen together.

'But why not a full passport?' asked Toogood.

'Easier to get,' said Gaffney. 'Less formality. You can get them at a post office or a DHSS office, and you don't have to have referees – you know, the person who signs the back of the photograph and says it's a good likeness.'

'And it's cheaper,' said Tipper.

'D'you mean that you can just walk in and get one of these things?'

'More or less,' said Gaffney. 'I think you have to produce something to prove your identity – birth certificate, driving licence.'

'How would he do that?'

'Have you read *The Day of the Jackal*?' asked Tipper.

'Ah, yes, of course.' Toogood hesitated. 'But how d'you check?'

'I suspect the answer to that is we don't,' said Gaffney. 'For the very simple reason that we don't know what we're looking for – or more particularly, who we're looking for. I don't know where they store the forms, but even if it's centrally it would take months, going through photographs, and even then we might not find him. You'd have to use searchers who knew what Mallory looked like, and he'd only have had to wear glasses, or comb his hair differently, and that would throw them completely.'

'D'you know what I'd've done in his place?' asked Tipper, reflectively. 'Assuming that she's got a passport in her own name – either Lambert or Gaston, but it's probably Lambert; if I'd been Mallory, I'd have gone as Mr Lambert. It looks better, doesn't it? Husband and wife, travelling together. No questions. No discerning glances from immigration officers and the rest. Nothing to cause anybody to remember them.'

Gaffney pondered on that. 'But supposing Lambert – the real Lambert – has got a passport already?'

201

'He almost certainly has,' said Tipper. 'When I interviewed him, he said that he was a computer salesman, and that he travelled a lot. He was talking about foreign porn magazines at the time.'

'Then he'd have a full passport – the blue hard-bound job.'

'I suppose so – we could always check.'

'That rules that out then,' said Toogood.

'Doesn't, you know,' said Tipper. 'I'll bet you they never check on anyone who goes into a post office and gets a BVP. They might do the occasional spot check, but the assumption is that anyone who applies for a BVP hasn't got a full passport. Anyway, by the time they've discovered it's fraudulent, it's usually too late. Duff address, false name – no trace; forget it, they'll say.'

'But how would he verify it?' asked Gaffney.

'Could do it a variety of ways, I should think. But isn't it worth a go, sir? I could get somebody in C1 Passports to run a check on James Lambert, unless your contacts can do it quicker?' He looked at Toogood.

'I doubt it,' said the MI5 man. 'Anyway, if it does turn up, you'd need it as evidence, wouldn't you?'

'Yes, that's true. Right,' he said to Gaffney, 'Leave it to me, guv'nor; I'll get someone to do it.'

It took time. But it was positive. A post office in Camden Town had issued a British Visitors Passport on Friday, the twenty-second of August, to one James Lambert, who had produced a provisional driving licence to support his application. Detectives from C1 Passport Squad had checked the driving licence: the address was false, and the real James Lambert already possessed a full licence. But the photograph, probably taken in a booth on a railway station somewhere, was Robert Mallory – wearing glasses.

'I think Master Mallory's going to have a bit of explaining to do,' said Gaffney mildly.

Chapter Eighteen

It is a popular myth that policemen favour executing search warrants at five o'clock in the morning. It is not true; policemen, in common with most people, detest getting up early. That is not to say that it doesn't sometimes happen; there can be a distinct advantage in it, particularly when common criminals are involved, because the circumstances demand it. Common criminals, if they work at all, usually go to work early, frequently stay away from home all day, and spend their evenings in public houses, returning only at closing time, and in an alcoholic stupor. Indeed, the storming of a dwelling in the early hours gives the police a tactical advantage, involving, as it often does, the breaking down of doors with a sledge-hammer – known in the trade as a seven pound key – and the sudden influx of officers, some of whom these days are, of necessity, armed. A man with a hangover faced with such aggressive visitors is, to say the least, handicapped.

None of these considerations however, applied in the case of Robert Mallory; a senior official of the Foreign and Commonwealth Office hardly came into the category of common criminal, even if he was suspected of murder.

Because of the Official Secrets Act implications, Gaffney and Tipper decided that it should be a joint operation. A Special Branch surveillance operation had been mounted, but only so that Gaffney and his team could be certain that Mallory was at home when they visited him. The Bow Street magistrate had been seen that morning in his chambers, before the court sat, and had granted a search warrant to Detective Chief Inspector Terry Dobbs upon his information that Robert Mallory was believed to have been engaged in 'acts preparatory' to the commission of an offence under the Act.

At seven o'clock the same evening, a number of unmarked police cars drew silently into Chalfont St Giles and stopped outside the Mallorys' elegant home. The surveillance team had reported that Robert Mallory and Lady Francesca were at home. Tessa was out.

The large double-fronted house lay back from the road, an adequacy of ground surrounding it, and at the back, French doors gave onto a patio and a swimming-pool, around which the Mallorys often entertained in the summer.

Gaffney and Tipper walked up the gravel drive, and as a precaution, two detective constables skirted the sides of the house to cater for the unlikely event of Mallory running away. It was a remote possibility, but experienced officers like Gaffney and Tipper knew that if the unthinkable happened, there would be no acceptable excuse for not having considered that it might just happen.

It was Lady Francesca who answered the door, and the policemen realised immediately that they were about to disrupt a social engagement of some importance. She was wearing a floor-length scarlet gown – Gaffney knew instinctively that the watered silk would rustle when she walked – with a large *diamanté* clasp on its silver belt. Her black hair was short and swept back, and she wore no jewellery. She looked at the two detectives and her whole body radiated disdain: she knew she was dealing with social inferiors.

'Yes?'

'Mr Mallory, please. We're police officers.'

'I'm his wife. What is it about?' She didn't move, but held the door firmly ajar with her left hand. 'We're about to go out; he won't have time to see you now. I suggest that you make an appointment to see him at the Foreign Office tomorrow; that's where he normally deals with business matters.' She was even more haughty when she spoke.

'It is not a Foreign Office matter, Lady Francesca.' She looked slightly surprised to be correctly addressed. 'And I'm afraid that we must insist on seeing him now.'

'Out of the question. Anyway, he's not here.'

'I happen to know that he is,' said Gaffney, his patience now starting to fray a little. 'We have had him under observation.'

'This is monstrous,' said Lady Francesca. 'I shall speak to your Commissioner about it; I'm seeing him later this evening.'

If only you knew what little impact that sort of threat had, thought Gaffney. Anyway, she might be seeing the Commissioner, but it was a racing certainty that her husband wouldn't. Gaffney had had enough. He withdrew the single sheet of paper from his pocket. 'I have a warrant to search these premises, Lady Francesca, and if you refuse to admit us, then I shall have no alternative but to enter forcibly – as this warrant empowers me to do.'

'My God,' she said, her face draining of colour, not from fear but from fury. She relinquished her hold on the door and retreated. 'Robert,' she called. 'Come here, quickly.'

Robert Mallory appeared through a door at the back of the spacious hallway. He was attired in full evening dress, a cluster of miniature medals on his left lapel, and he absently twisted at his signet ring as he strode towards the front door.

'What is it?' He lifted his head as he spoke, looking down his nose in an imperious way so theatrical that it was almost comical. Then he recognised the policemen. 'What's

205

the meaning of this? You should come to the office if you want to see me.'

Gaffney was getting just a little weary of this charade. 'I have a warrant to search your house under the Official Secrets Act,' he said. 'It was granted by the Bow Street magistrate this morning.'

Suddenly the pomposity went out of Mallory. He took a handkerchief from his pocket and dabbed at his forehead. 'You'd better come in,' he said in a resigned tone.

At a signal from Tipper, four more police officers came quickly up the drive – among them Detective Sergeant Claire Wentworth and Charles Markham – and waited in the hallway, gazing round at the opulence of a property they knew would never come within the scope of their rent allowance.

'What do these people want?' asked Lady Francesca, clearly unwilling to surrender without a fight.

'They are going to search the house, madam,' said Tipper.

'But – look, Robert . . . '

Mallory looked crossly at his wife. 'Just let me deal with this, will you,' he said sharply. 'And I suggest that you go and get changed; I doubt that we'll be going out tonight.'

'But— '

He turned his back on her and addressed himself to Gaffney. 'What exactly is this all about, Superintendent?'

Gaffney gauged that there was now nothing to lose by a correction. 'Chief Superintendent,' he said, emphasising the first word.

'Yes – Chief Superintendent,' said Mallory injecting a similar stress. 'What do you want?' He turned to watch his wife regally ascending the stairs, and Gaffney noted that the dress did indeed rustle. 'Perhaps we should go into the study.' He realigned his gaze on the policeman.

'I think that might be a good idea,' said Gaffney.

It was the sort of study that Gaffney had always wanted to have, but knew that he would never be able to afford.

Book-lined and richly carpeted, with a large desk across one corner, and a brass lamp casting a pool of light on the tooled leather top.

It was behind this desk that Mallory now seated himself. He waved a hand, limply, towards the two hide armchairs. 'You'd better sit down. Would you like a drink?'

'Thank you, no,' said Gaffney, speaking for himself and Tipper.

'D'you mind if I do?' Mallory reached towards the decanter on the edge of the desk and paused.

It was unusual, but this was an unusual affair, and more might be gained from allowing Mallory to have the whisky he clearly so urgently needed at that moment. 'Go ahead.'

Steadily, without the slightest indication of a shaking hand, Mallory poured a measure of Scotch into a chunky crystal tumbler. Slowly he lifted it, took a sip and set it down again. 'Well?' He was beginning to recover some of his poise.

'How often did you see Eva van Heem?' asked Gaffney.

Mallory smiled bleakly. 'So that's it.' He looked down at his glass, his hand over the top, slowly rotating it, back and forth. 'How can you be so sure that I saw her at all?' he asked.

'You were seen to meet her in a public house in Mornington Crescent about four weeks ago.' Gaffney held Mallory's gaze unblinkingly. 'About five feet nine inches, short brown hair, wearing white jeans and a navy blue sweater. Lives in Hendon.'

Mallory nodded wearily. 'It's not an offence to meet a woman in a pub, you know – even if she is a South African diplomat.'

'Why then did you deny it – when we last spoke?'

For the first time, Mallory showed a flash of annoyance. 'Use your common sense, man – I'm married.' Then he recovered. 'I'm sorry – this has all come as a surprise.'

The door of the study opened; in contrast to the finery she had been wearing when the police arrived, Lady

Francesca was now wearing faded blue jeans and a navy guernsey. 'These people are all over the house,' she said. There was outrage in her voice. 'Robert – did you hear me?' Gaffney's woman sergeant hovered in the doorway behind Mallory's wife.

'Yes, I heard you. Just let them get on with it and don't interfere.'

'Well – really, Robert. Courtesy costs nothing.' She turned her gaze on Gaffney. 'I'm going out,' she announced. 'I presume you've no objection to that, officer. Or are you going to arrest me?'

Gaffney stood up and turned to face her. She really was most attractive, even when she was angry – perhaps because she was angry. 'No objection at all, Lady Francesca.'

For a moment she surveyed the three men in the room, then without another word, she turned and left. It was the last time that Robert Mallory ever saw her.

'Were you having an affair with the van Heem woman?'

For a moment it looked as though Mallory was going to object to the question. Then he spoke quietly. 'Yes, I was.'

Gaffney wasn't convinced of that. 'How often did you see her – on average?'

Mallory laughed. 'On average? There was no average. I only saw her four times. That time in Mornington Crescent was the first meeting.' He smiled at some arcane memory. 'We didn't go to bed that day, as I'm sure you will know.' He hesitated, and then, looking straight at Gaffney said, 'She was trying to blackmail me, you know.'

Gaffney was fairly certain he knew how, but he asked just the same.

'I got a telephone call at the office one day – out of the blue, asking me to meet her.'

'And you went – just like that?'

'Yes. We're not exactly an intelligence organisation – my part of the Office, but we do occasionally get information from some rather strange sources, so it didn't occur to me not to go.'

Gaffney didn't believe that for a moment, but refrained from saying so.

'So I went,' continued Mallory. 'I must admit I was astounded by the sheer brazenness of the woman. She didn't hesitate for a moment. She calmly announced that she knew I was having an affair with my secretary, hinted that if it got out I wouldn't get the K I'm due for, and then proceeded to list the information she wanted.'

'What did you say?'

'I'm afraid I laughed. I don't quite think that that was the reaction she expected. I told her that dozens of men had affairs with their secretaries, and that I certainly wasn't going to become a spy to preserve a knighthood. One never gets away with it, so considered logically, it is counter-productive. You finish up losing all round.'

To Gaffney that sounded like diplomatic mumbo-jumbo. 'Who is the secretary?'

Mallory played for time. 'Oughtn't you to have cautioned me?'

Gaffney smiled. 'Only if and when I think you have committed an offence,' he said.

'I take it that we can keep this between ourselves, Mr – er, Gaffney, isn't it?'

'Yes, it is. And no – I can't give you any undertaking of that nature, as I'm sure you must know, Mr Mallory.'

'Kate McLaren.'

Gaffney knew that was true. 'And how long has that been going on?'

'Some months, actually.' Mallory smoothed his hand over the desk top and took another sip of whisky.

'But she'd only been your secretary for a matter of weeks, surely? Since Mrs Lambert's resignation.'

Mallory smiled blandly. 'That's why she became my secretary, Mr Gaffney.'

That may or may not have been true. Mallory certainly wasn't going to admit to having had an affair with Mrs Lambert – not yet anyway. He switched back to Eva van Heem. 'How did it come about then that you finished up having an affair with a woman who set out to blackmail you?'

'I'm afraid that some women find me irresistible,' he said without any trace of vanity. 'I can't explain it, it's just a fact of life.'

You conceited bastard, thought Harry Tipper, who had been watching the exchange with a mixture of astonishment and grudging admiration. Astonishment because he had never met a man who could be so cool under interrogation, even cloaked as it was in the guise of an urbane conversation. Both Mallory and Gaffney knew it was nothing of the sort, but Tipper was beginning to understand something of the talents that were needed to make a success of the Diplomatic Service.

Gaffney grinned. 'Are you saying to me, Mr Mallory, that from a first meeting with Miss van Heem when, on your own admission, she attempted to put the black on you – that from that first meeting, by the second you were in bed with her?'

'Yes – quite simply, Mr Gaffney. That is it exactly.'

'I'm interested to know just how you managed to achieve that.'

'Well I insisted that we should have no further meetings in insalubrious public houses – I don't normally frequent such places. I said that I would think about her proposition, and that I would come and see her at her home. And I did.'

'How did you know where she lived?'

Mallory looked pitifully at the policeman. 'I do work at the Foreign Office,' he said.

'Yes, of course.'

'And so I went to Hendon about three days later. I told her that I had alerted MI5, and that they knew where I was – had in fact accompanied me there, but that they were going to do nothing about her approach provided that she made no further attempts to suborn me. She had the good grace to admit defeat and, well, one thing led to another . . . '

'You hadn't alerted MI5, of course?'

'Come now, Chief Superintendent. You are Special Branch, I presume? You would know perfectly well that I hadn't spoken to them. I couldn't possibly afford to.'

'I don't see why not. If this woman was trying to put some pressure on you to commit a serious offence, the Security Service and ourselves would have dealt with it, firmly.'

'Oh, I've no doubt. But the Director-General of the Security Service would have been duty-bound to tell the Head of the Foreign Office, and that would have been that.'

There was a tap at the study door, and Tipper walked across and opened it. There was a brief conversation and he walked back to Gaffney. 'This room needs to be searched, sir,' he said to him.

'Tell them to come in,' said Mallory magnanimously.

For the next ten minutes conversation was suspended as the two officers who had been assigned to searching the study went methodically about their task. Mallory sat back in his chair calmly drinking from his recharged whisky tumbler, apparently secure in the knowledge that these clumsy policemen would find nothing.

Gaffney, too, sat calmly watching them. He had seen it all before. The over-confidence that so often preceded disaster when a policeman found something that alone meant little, but only because the suspect was unaware that they had other evidence which, when put together with the find, made it suddenly significant. Gaffney smiled to himself: it was MI5's jigsaw syndrome again.

And then it happened. A detective constable – a young man, with only four years' service, and two of those walking a beat – opened a small reproduction antique cabinet upon which rested a silver gallery tray and some glasses – the companions to the one from which Mallory was drinking. Inside the cabinet was a safe. 'Would you open this, please, sir,' said the detective.

'I'm afraid I can't do that,' said Mallory.

'You mean you don't have the key?' asked Gaffney.

'I have the key, but it contains certain secret Foreign Office documents. I'm sure you will understand, Chief Superintendent, that— '

'May I use your telephone?' asked Gaffney mildly.

'Of course.' The self-confidence was still there.

'I suppose you don't know Sir John Laker's telephone number off hand, do you?' Gaffney asked. 'It'll save me bothering the Resident Clerk at the Foreign Office.'

'What do you want his number for?' There was an edge to Mallory's voice, now that the Head of the Diplomatic Service had been mentioned.

'Because I shall need him to come here – now – to be present when that safe is opened.' Gaffney remained seated and relaxed. 'If, as you say, it contains Foreign Office documents, I don't suppose he'll be too happy at the prospect of their being kept in a private house – in a safe or not.'

Mallory put his hand in his trousers pocket, and by way of an answer threw a bunch of keys on to the leather top of the desk. He said nothing, but his stature seemed to have diminished slightly, and Gaffney thought that he now looked faintly ridiculous in his white tie and tail-coat.

Tipper, who had seen the reactions of some people to the finding of damning evidence, decided that he would prefer not to have a desk between him and Mallory. The film-maker's favourite scene of the suspect withdrawing a pistol from the drawer of a desk was not likely to occur here, but it always paid never to take chances – just in case. 'Would you mind coming round here, Mr Mallory.'

Mallory raised a quizzical eyebrow, but started to walk round the desk.

'It's just that I would prefer you to witness what is taken out of your safe.'

The young detective removed two or three jewel boxes and handed them to a colleague who put them on a side table. Then he opened a shallow drawer at the bottom and withdrew an envelope – a government issue envelope. He handed it to Gaffney. 'And there's this, sir,' he said, passing over a video tape.

Gaffney walked over to the desk and emptied the contents of the envelope on to its leather top. There were six half-plate prints, and six negatives which Gaffney presumed matched. The photographs were of Mallory and Penelope Lambert engaging in several variations of the sexual act, most of which would probably have been described as disgustingly obscene by any member of the judiciary you cared to mention. He was pretty certain he knew what was on the tape.

Gaffney looked up. Mallory was staring at the photographs as if mesmerised. 'You knew these were there, of course?'

Mallory nodded blankly.

'In the act,' said Gaffney drily. 'There's a Latin phrase for it, but I can never remember it.'

'*In flagrante delicto*,' murmured Mallory.

Chapter Nineteen

Gaffney had suggested that Mallory got changed before they took him to the police station, and he had put on a sports jacket, cavalry twills and a polo-necked sweater. Gaffney left two officers behind to keep the search warrant open, but Mallory had insisted on showing them how to set the burglar alarm in case, he said, they left before he got back. The irony of that caused Claire Wentworth to disappear into the kitchen to have a private fit of the giggles.

Gaffney, Tipper and Mallory sat now in the interview room of Cannon Row police station in the shadow of the old Scotland Yard, abandoned to politicians by the Metropolitan Police in 1967.

While the police had been searching the house at Chalfont, another contribution to the demise of Robert Mallory had arrived. The gendarmerie, to their credit, had carried out a thorough scientific examination of the house in St Brouille where Penelope Lambert had stayed. One of the fingerprints which they had found, but not identified, was compared with Mallory's, and when Gaffney had arrived at Cannon Row there was a message waiting for him from the senior fingerprint officer. They matched: and it was not portable evidence as the camera had been. The case was getting stronger.

Tipper had cautioned him, which Mallory wrongly assumed to be a routine part of arriving at a police station. But it was Tipper's next statement which dismayed him. 'You stayed

214

with Mrs Penelope Lambert at a house known as Seventeen Rue de la Digue in St Brouille in Northern France on Saturday the twenty-third of August and Sunday the twenty-fourth.'

The sudden change in police interest from Eva van Heem – an almost friendly and sympathetic approach – to Penelope Lambert, seriously rattled Mallory.

'What on earth are you talking about?'

'Your fingerprints were found in the house, Mr Mallory.'

'I don't see— '

'Furthermore, Mr Mallory, the letter of resignation which she submitted to her employers – the Foreign Office – was in all probability typed on the portable typewriter found at your house. That machine has been taken to the Forensic Science Laboratory where tests will be carried out, but I don't think that there is any doubt, do you?'

'She asked me to type it for her.'

'Why? She was a competent typist, and she had a typewriter in her office.' He went on, relentlessly. 'And there was no trace of her fingerprints on the letter. Strange that, don't you think?'

Mallory opened his mouth to say something, thought better of it, and remained silent.

'I suggest, Mr Mallory, that you forged that letter of resignation – we are fairly satisfied that it was not her signature – and that you then obtained a false passport . . . ' With a flourish, he produced the application form which the police had obtained from the authorities, and laid the photograph of Mallory, wearing glasses and purporting to be James Lambert, on the table between them. 'That you then accompanied Mrs Lambert to France where you murdered her.' He leaned back in his chair.

'Murdered her? What do you mean?'

'Exactly what I say.'

'She drowned.'

'Really? Perhaps you would care to tell me about it.'

215

Mallory appeared to be taking stock of his position, but Tipper was now familiar enough with the man to know that his brain was racing madly, trying desperately to think of a counter to this latest twist that threatened him.

'I admit I've been foolish,' he said at length. 'Very foolish. But it was a difficult situation – of my own making, certainly, and looking back, I should never have done it. It was just a bit of excitement. It was for the sex – nothing else. But then she started talking about marriage. I could see her point of view, being divorced and everything – wanting some permanency, some security, but we were just not compatible – except in bed. We really hit it off there.' He smiled at the recollection. 'It was later on on the Sunday evening – about nine o'clock it must have been, and she started on again about getting married. We had a blazing row – nothing violent – we didn't come to blows; we were neither of us like that.

'Finally she swept out of the room and went into the bedroom. I just sat there – regretting. Regretting having started the whole thing – regretting having come to France. Anyway she came back into the room. She was wearing her bikini, well the bottom half – it's quite normal there. She had a towelling robe on, just over her shoulders, and she was carrying a towel. She said she was going for a swim to cool off. I should have stopped her, I suppose. We'd both been drinking fairly heavily – a lot of wine through the day – then more with dinner, and a few brandies when we got in. I wouldn't say that we were drunk, but I wouldn't have driven a car.

'Anyway, she went off – just across the road to the beach, I imagined, because she didn't take the car – it was still outside later on. After about an hour, I started to get a bit worried, and I'd calmed down by then. I walked over the road to look for her. The beach was deserted. No one. There was no sign of her. No one in the water and I couldn't see her towel or her robe anywhere. I just didn't

216

know what had happened to her. I walked the full length of the beach, along the waterline, looking for her and calling out. It was quite dark then, but I couldn't see or hear anything of her.

'I must admit I panicked then. I didn't want to raise the alarm – I would have had to face the publicity – my wife, the Office. And if she had drowned it would have been too late for me to do anything. I sat up half the night wondering what to do, hoping that she'd turn up. I eventually dozed off in the armchair.

'I suppose I woke up about eight o'clock the next morning. There was still no sign of her. I went across to the beach again and searched for her robe and towel, but I didn't find them. I went back to the house and gathered up her things – there weren't many – we'd both travelled light – and took them with me. I suppose I took a chance, but you don't think very clearly in circumstances like that. I just left them on one of the luggage racks on the ferry.'

Tipper nodded slowly, as if he had accepted all that Mallory had been saying. 'This car you mentioned – where did that come from?'

'We'd hired it – or rather Penny had. I didn't have a licence you see.'

'Not in your own name, just the provisional one you obtained in the name of James Lambert to support your application for the false passport.'

'You know about that?'

'Of course. But what happened to the car?'

'I didn't want to leave it there, so I drove it to the garage where she'd hired it from, and left it outside. There was nothing to pay.'

'And the camera? What about the film in the camera?'

'That had a photograph of me on it. I couldn't very well leave that, could I?' He smiled, a trace of the old contempt still there. 'I took it out before I packed her things and threw it overboard during the crossing.'

217

'And then you just came back to this country and went to work as if nothing had happened?'

'Yes, I'm afraid so. It wasn't a very noble thing to do, but there was nothing tangible that I could contribute, was there? She had just gone – without a trace.'

'But still you didn't think to tell anybody – the authorities, the police for instance? And when I came to see you, you still didn't see fit to mention it. Now why was that, Mr Mallory?'

'It was obviously too late then, wasn't it?' There was an almost supercilious sneer on Mallory's face now, as though he constantly despaired of the dull-wittedness of policemen. 'There was absolutely nothing I could do to bring her back. As I thought – she had drowned. It was still a shock, when I read it in the newspaper.' Mallory's confidence was clearly fast returning, and Tipper thought, grudgingly, what a resilient man he was.

'Have you ever heard of George Joseph Smith?' asked Tipper conversationally.

'Er – no, I don't think so. Should I have done?' He raised an eyebrow as if Tipper were talking about someone who might have worked in the Foreign Office at some time.

'You see, Mr Mallory, Mrs Lambert did not drown – she was murdered. Probably by someone seizing her ankles while she was taking a bath. One of the mistakes that George Joseph Smith made, way back in nineteen-fifteen, was to assume that death in those cases is caused by drowning. It's not. It's what those clever pathologists call vagal inhibition. To laymen – like you and me – the best way of describing it is shock – a paralysis of the central nervous system.' He paused for effect. 'It was you who seized her ankles, Mr Mallory, so sharply that her head went under the water immediately, and the water went straight up her nostrils and she was dead. You then dragged her out of the bath, attired her in the bottom half of her bikini – nice touch that; local colour I suppose you'd call it – and put her body

218

in the car and drove it to Le Roc Dent. Then you pitched her over thinking she'd be lost forever.

'Unfortunately, the tides are such that she fetched up practically on the doorstep of the very house you had killed her in. The gendarmerie could have told you that would happen. Well they could now – they've done a lot of work on it.'

Mallory looked stunned; his face ashen.

But Tipper refused to relent – gave him no time to collect his thoughts. 'Mr John Wallace who, you will recall, was arrested a few days ago under the Official Secrets Act, has been extremely helpful to us.' Tipper tapped the envelope containing the photographs that had been taken from Mallory's safe earlier that evening. 'And he admits to having taken these. That's why we knew what we were looking for. He took them on the seventeenth of June and obligingly recorded the fact in his diary. So, incidentally, did she. He gave her a set of the prints, but he kept the negatives. You obviously didn't know at the time that they were being taken – you were busy; very busy. But you soon found out when Mrs Lambert started putting the pressure on – and gave you a set of the prints. But she was under pressure too. The video tape we seized from your house – and you're obviously familiar with the contents – was recorded on Eva van Heem's instructions, by a South African agent called Webster. But there was another tape – of Penny and van Heem. That tape had been used by van Heem to blackmail Penny. There was ample evidence that Penny was bi-sexual, and she had had a lesbian relationship of a permanent nature, but it was probably not known at the Foreign Office – in fact, almost certainly not; it would have prejudiced her positive vetting. And that was the lever that Eva van Heem used. Eva, however, from what we hear, was pure lesbian, so your suggestion that you had had an affair with her is, to say the least, suspect. But all she wanted was to marry you, wasn't it?' He gave Mallory no time to answer.

219

'Her mistake was to give the negatives to John Wallace to take care of – or rather – to leave them with him. She never actually had them. But you knew what John Wallace was doing for Eva van Heem – I've got to give you credit for that, turning the tables on a professional, and getting her to give you information. So you leaned on Wallace and got him to hand over the negatives. But there was one little doubt, wasn't there? There might just have been a set of these photographs still in Penny's flat – and you had to make sure. But you had no idea where the original of the tape was. That was your first call on your return, wasn't it?' Tipper paused. 'You see, we never found her house keys – not in her luggage, and obviously not on the body.'

'You can't prove any of it,' said Mallory, his voice rising in pitch.

Tipper knew differently. 'But apart from all that, Mr Mallory, you said just now that you awoke from your doze at about eight o'clock the following morning – the morning after Mrs Lambert's disappearance – apparently while swimming.'

Mallory nodded.

'Unfortunately, Mr Mallory, her body was found about two hours before that, in the cold light of dawn. And you were already on the ferry – in fact, were very close by then to Portsmouth, having quite deliberately left the night before, immediately after disposing of her body. You didn't go out to look the next morning. You couldn't have done – you weren't there, and you knew there'd be no point.'

Mallory went to say something, but Tipper held up his hand and went on.

'You admit having left her luggage on the ferry that docked about one hour after the discovery of her body, and about one hour before you supposedly woke up and went to look for her. You would have seen the activity – the gendarmerie, the photographers, wouldn't you? And they would possibly have seen you?' That was a guess.

'Incidentally, that luggage contained Mrs Lambert's beach robe, the one you said she was wearing when you last saw her – or had you forgotten?'

Mallory stared at the detective, his face grey. The lines around his mouth were deep-etched and he suddenly looked older than his years – much older. For a moment he said nothing. The drive had gone. The ingenuity of his training had dissipated. The twisting and turning upon which he had seemed, at times, to thrive, was now exhausted. At long last Tipper saw before him a broken man.

At length Mallory spoke. 'The very first day she became my secretary I knew that I had to have her. She was provocative. She wore clothes that were designed to be attractive – sexually, I mean. I tried to stop her – to stop the inevitable. I remember she started wearing a leather skirt, very thin and very tight. I told her she shouldn't come to work in it, that it wasn't quite the thing for the Foreign Office. She pouted at me and said that it was, after all, a skirt – it was not as if she had come in trousers. She knew there was a rule about trousers.

'She knew all about me – these girls gossip with each other, you know. She knew that I was going off to another ambassador's post somewhere, and she must have known I was about due for a K, too. But the mistake I made, the first serious mistake, was to take her with me to Brussels. It was a conference – one of those endless EEC things. A lot of people take their secretaries – quite properly of course. There's nothing underhand about it, and my wife knew. And the Office allows for it – expenses, I mean. It was that first night that she did for me – in a sense. She'd been making the running all along, but that night she clinched it. She just walked into my room, undressed, and got into bed with me. She never spoke a word.'

'You could have thrown her out – there and then, surely? Sent her straight back to London?'

Mallory looked unbelievingly at Tipper. 'What would that have achieved? They might have believed it – back here, but there would have been a few who wouldn't. And what about her? Think of the wild allegations she could have made – victim of a senior official's lust – attempted rape! She'd refused my advances, so I sent her home, trying to make it look as though it was the other way round. She'd have had great fun with that.

'It was all too easy. After that it became a regular thing. Hampton Wick was too awkward, and I persuaded her to move in a bit. Eventually we found this place at Wimbledon and I helped her with the expenses, because she was always short of money.'

Tipper smiled, thinking of the four thousand pounds she had had in her bank account.

'But then she started threatening. She wanted me to leave Francesca and marry her. She actually said that she would like to be an ambassador's wife – to be Lady Mallory. It started to get obvious. She would call me "darling" at the Office – only when the two of us were there, but it was a hint that she could and would do it anytime she felt like it. And she said that she would tell people. She even threatened to ring up Francesca and tell her. I didn't know what the hell to do. You can't sack people in the Foreign Office – well not like you can in industry. I thought about getting her transferred to another department, but I knew that that would be no good either – and I think she guessed. She said that if I had her moved she would blow the whistle on me.' He frowned, an expression of distaste on his face. 'That was the actual expression she used: blow the whistle.'

Mallory leaned forward on the table resting on his folded arms. 'It was marriage she wanted, and she drove me so hard that I even considered it at one stage. But it would have been a messy divorce. Francesca's not the sort of woman you walk out on. She'd have dumped me without a thought, of that I'm quite sure, but she'd never have stood for me

222

leaving her. And she's got friends in high places. She could have ruined me, utterly. I tried to explain all this to Penny but she thought I was making excuses. She wasn't awfully bright, I'm afraid.'

Mallory leaned back in his chair and suddenly smiled; it was uncharacteristic – ghoulish almost. 'Then Eva van Heem sent for me, and told me that she knew all about the affair and gave me a copy of the tape of Penny and me. The same day, a coincidence I think, Penny brought a set of the photographs to work with her. She put them in an envelope, walked into my office and just handed them to me without a word. I knew I was done for. I worked out how I could kill her without leaving a trace – or so I thought!'

Tipper nodded. 'Is there anything else you wish to say, Mr Mallory?'

'I should like to send for my solicitor,' he said quietly.

The French authorities surrendered their right to extradite Robert Mallory, even though a murder committed on the sovereign soil of France is usually tried there. But this was the murder of an Englishwoman by an Englishman, her lover, and both were domiciled in England. English law caters for it adequately. A British subject may be tried at the Old Bailey for a crime committed anywhere in the world – and so he was. Which was a pity really. In France Mallory would probably have escaped lightly because of the lenient view the French take of what they quaintly term 'crime passionnel'.

Three months later, Robert Mallory, whom ironically the other prisoners called 'Sir' Robert – even though his Sovereign never did – was found hanged in his cell in the lifers' block at Parkhurst. One of the first inmates of the prison to hear of it was John Wallace, serving fourteen years for espionage.